SCAN. ᴋLEY

FENELLA J MILLER

B
Boldwood

First published in 2015 as *A Scandal at Pemberley*. This edition published in Great Britain in 2024 by Boldwood Books Ltd.

Copyright © Fenella J. Miller, 2015

Cover Design by Colin Thomas

Cover Images: Colin Thomas and Shutterstock

The moral right of Fenella J. Miller to be identified as the author of this work has been asserted in accordance with the Copyright, Designs and Patents Act 1988.

All rights reserved. No part of this book may be reproduced in any form or by any electronic or mechanical means, including information storage and retrieval systems, without written permission from the author, except for the use of brief quotations in a book review. This book is a work of fiction and, except in the case of historical fact, any resemblance to actual persons, living or dead, is purely coincidental.

Every effort has been made to obtain the necessary permissions with reference to copyright material, both illustrative and quoted. We apologise for any omissions in this respect and will be pleased to make the appropriate acknowledgements in any future edition.

A CIP catalogue record for this book is available from the British Library.

Paperback ISBN 978-1-83518-732-6

Large Print ISBN 978-1-83518-733-3

Hardback ISBN 978-1-83518-731-9

Ebook ISBN 978-1-83518-734-0

Kindle ISBN 978-1-83518-735-7

Audio CD ISBN 978-1-83518-726-5

MP3 CD ISBN 978-1-83518-727-2

Digital audio download ISBN 978-1-83518-730-2

This book is printed on certified sustainable paper. Boldwood Books is dedicated to putting sustainability at the heart of our business. For more information please visit https://www.boldwoodbooks.com/about-us/sustainability/

Boldwood Books Ltd, 23 Bowerdean Street, London, SW6 3TN

www.boldwoodbooks.com

1

'My word, one would never know that anything untoward had taken place at Pemberley,' Bingley exclaimed as he looked at the front of the house.

'The workmen have done a splendid job repairing the windows and the damage to the interior where necessary,' Darcy replied as he held his hand out to Lizzy.

'Ours will be the first Darcy baby born under this roof for more than a hundred years.' Lizzy took her husband's hand, no doubt glad of the support as the ground was decidedly slippery. 'We have been fortunate with the weather this winter; no snow since January, and already the daffodils and snowdrops are in bud.'

Georgiana had mixed feelings about their return to the family home. Living at the Old Rectory, as Adam's house was now called, had been most enjoyable. Major Jonathan Brownstone – Adam's friend – had proved to be an entertaining gentleman, and she was sad she would no longer be able to spend time with him.

He had been staying at Pemberley when the ghosts had

departed so dramatically and had remained to help with the move to the Old Rectory. Unfortunately, he had been obliged to return to his regiment shortly afterwards and she had not seen him again until he had arrived two days ago to stand as groomsman to Adam when he and Kitty celebrated their marriage next week.

'Come along, Georgiana, you are wool-gathering. I am eager to be able to walk about Pemberley without fear of being accosted by a ghost.'

'Kitty dearest, did you hear that Fitzwilliam intends to have the east wing turned into a permanent home for Jane and Bingley? He has already instructed the architects, and the work will be starting as soon as the weather is clement.' She had only discovered this exciting piece of news herself that morning and was delighted Jane would not now be moving to another establishment.

'That is wonderful. I shall be living no more than three miles from here, so we will be able to spend delightful afternoons together at the Old Rectory or here.'

Georgiana grabbed her friend's hand and they ran into the house to join in the general exclamations of praise and surprise that the damage done by the departing spectres had been so easily restored. She wished to speak privately to Kitty at the earliest possible opportunity and the only place where they could do this was in the apartment they shared.

'Fitzwilliam, Kitty and I are going to check her bride clothes. Are we to dress for dinner tonight?' Georgiana asked her brother.

'Yes, of course. King and Brownstone will be joining us and it's to be a celebration. I believe it's possible Mr and Mrs Bennet, Mrs Wickham and Miss Bennet might also arrive this afternoon.' He grinned at Lizzy. 'No doubt your parents will expect the formalities to be maintained, whatever our views on the matter.'

Lizzy returned his smile. 'There is no need to prevaricate, my love. We all know it is my mother who is a stickler for the niceties of etiquette. My father does not give a fig for such things.'

Jane and Lizzy, followed by their respective husbands, strolled off to the small drawing room, which was the warmest room in this enormous establishment. Georgiana was bursting with her news but knew better than to discuss anything of an intimate nature where a member of staff might overhear.

The Great Stairs had not been used by the family for some time and she was reluctant to take the first step. Three men had died here, crushed by falling timber, and she was concerned that there might still be ghosts on the premises.

'All of the ghosts have gone, Georgiana. It is perfectly safe to take this route. Indeed, I have every intention of exploring the east wing for myself before the workmen start the renovations. Shall we go up together? I promise you there are no phantoms at Pemberley now.'

'Well, as you were the one who could speak to them directly, I must take your word for it.' Georgiana ran up the first few marble steps and stopped, took a deep breath, and her fear vanished. 'The house does feel quite different. As I told you before, I have never felt quite comfortable here and was always happier spending time away. Now, I do believe Pemberley is a friendly place.'

Without further hesitation she held her skirts up and ran to the gallery. The feeble February sunlight flickered through the new glass of the enormous windows and made patterns on the polished boards. Kitty joined her and, snatching her hands, began to twirl her around the floor. Breathless and happy, they dashed down the wide passageway and into their shared apartment. She was really going to miss her bosom bow when Kitty left next week as the wife of Adam King, the former rector of Bakewell.

Both their personal maids were busy elsewhere and they had the sitting room to themselves. Georgiana curled up in the nearest armchair and her friend flopped down on the *chaise longue* opposite. 'We are supposed to be checking your bride clothes, Kitty, but I'm quite certain Annie and Ellie have got the matter in hand. I wish to tell you something quite remarkable and you must promise not to breathe a word to anyone – especially to Adam.'

'I think I know what you are about to tell me, dearest one. You have feelings for Adam's dashing friend and I am quite certain he is equally interested in you.' Kitty smiled in a most particular way. 'Indeed, I think that you will have no need to tell anybody, as they have all guessed your secret.'

An unpleasant heat travelled from her toes to the crown of her head. 'Oh, do not say so! I cannot bear to think I have been so transparent in my regard for Major Brownstone.' She swallowed a lump in her throat. 'Do you think that Fitzwilliam is aware we are interested in each other?'

'He would have to have had his head in the clouds to have missed the way you and the handsome major have been looking at each other.'

'I liked him from the moment we were first introduced last December. He has an excellent pedigree, and although only a second son, his father is Lord Brownstone and his grandfather is an earl.'

'Does he have his own estate?' Kitty asked.

'Unfortunately he has only his bounty from his soldiering and his army pay. But that is of no matter; I have more than enough in my trust fund to keep us both in comfort. In fact, we will be able to purchase an estate in Derbyshire...' For a second time her face suffused with colour. 'Forgive me, I cannot imagine what made me say something so indecorous. I can assure you that there has been no mention of marriage or anything of that nature on either side. I was letting my imagination run away with me.'

'You are quite right to consider every element before consenting to a match – the fact that he has not yet asked you to be his bride is neither here nor there. No doubt he will speak to Darcy whilst he is here this time. I'm sure if your brother disapproved he would have stepped in before this and not allowed you to spend any time in Major Brownstone's company.'

Georgiana believed she had said too much already, even to her dearest friend. The major was a serving soldier and she had no wish to follow the drum. Unless he was prepared to resign his commission, the prospect of an engagement between them was remote.

'It is premature to talk of my becoming betrothed to him. I believe it is the fact that you are marrying after knowing Adam for such a short time that has put these ideas into my head. I have no intention of contracting an alliance with anyone until after I have had my Season.'

Kitty raised an eyebrow. 'I should think not. You do not have to make a decision on the matter until next year. Indeed, if it hadn't been for the dramatic events Adam and I became embroiled in, I doubt that we would have moved things on so rapidly. It was being in mortal danger that pushed us closer, and I do not regret my decision one jot.'

'Adam is the perfect match for you and I know you're going to be very happy married to him. I cannot tell you how relieved I am you are going to be living so close to me. You have become very dear since you came last year.'

'You will have both my sisters living here in future. I heard Lizzy say that Mary is to remain behind when my parents return to Longbourn.'

'I doubt that I will feel the same way about Mary. From what you have told me about her she is a bluestocking and not at all lively.'

'That is true, Georgiana, but one could have said the same about you before I arrived and now you are almost as effervescent as I. This time you must be the one to encourage Mary to relax and take life less seriously.'

The sound of someone moving about in the bedchamber next door halted the conversation. 'We had better go and check your wardrobe, just in case you need to borrow anything else from me. Please promise me you will not mention this conversation to anyone. Indeed, Kitty dearest, I should be eternally grateful if you would reassure Lizzy that I am not looking to become engaged to anyone at the moment. I am hoping she will tell Fitzwilliam not to approach the major.'

They had been happily engaged in admiring Kitty's many new gowns when a message came from downstairs summoning them, as the Bennet family had arrived. Georgiana was looking forward to meeting Kitty's family as she had heard much about them. Mr Bennet appeared to be a great favourite with Lizzy and Jane. Little had been said about Mary Bennet, but the one she most wished to meet was Lydia Wickham.

Lydia was the youngest of the Bennet sisters and, if gossip was to be believed, the wildest and the most beautiful. Fitzwilliam had stepped in and saved the girl's reputation when Wickham had run off with her and then failed to tie the knot. She shuddered at the thought of her own lucky escape from that scoundrel's clutches. He was *persona non grata* at Pemberley and for that she was profoundly grateful.

'We must go down, Kitty. Your family has arrived. I cannot tell you how eager I am to meet them all.'

Her friend pulled a comical face. 'I pray you do not change your mind once you have spent an hour or two in Mama's company. She has a good heart, but...'

'There is no need to apologise for your parent. You are fortunate to still have both of them.'

As they arrived at the gallery, Georgiana thought there must be a dozen or more people milling about in the lobby because of the cacophony of voices, the shrieks and laughter, which echoed up the Great Stairs. She paused and peeked over the balustrade, unexpectedly nervous about meeting the exuberant Bennet family.

'Come along, Georgiana, we are tardy and it has been far too long since my sisters and I have all been together. I cannot wait to introduce you and Adam to everyone.'

Before she could protest, Georgiana was unceremoniously bundled down the marble staircase to join the newcomers. The garrulous lady in a disturbingly large green bonnet could only be the redoubtable Mrs Bennet. Kitty led her across to be introduced.

'Mama, I am delighted to see you and Papa are here at last. I should like to introduce you to Miss Georgiana Darcy.'

This was a breach of protocol, as she should have been introduced to Mrs Bennet not the other way round. However, Kitty's mother seemed unbothered by this omission. She beamed and the clusters of fruit attached to the rim of her bonnet bobbed in a disconcerting way.

'My dear Miss Darcy, so kind of you to take my Kitty to your bosom. I fear that I am all of a tremble after so long a journey.

My nerves are in shreds, and I do declare it will be days before I am feeling myself again.' She gestured towards Mr Bennet, who was talking quietly to Lizzy and Jane. 'I told Mr Bennet how it would be, but he insisted that we continue our journey and arrive this afternoon when we could have stayed at a delightful post-house overnight and come tomorrow morning.'

Georgiana was bewildered by this rush of words but covered her confusion by curtsying. Fortunately, when she straightened Mrs Bennet had turned her attention to Bingley and she was free to step aside from the crush of people. Mr Bennet was a moderately tall gentleman with a fine head of dark brown hair, which had only a sprinkling of grey. She rather thought she might like him, for he had an intelligent face and kind eyes.

The tall, thin young lady, with her hair scraped back into an unattractive bun at the nape of her neck, must be Mary Bennet. Had she not borne a remarkable similarity to Lizzy and Kitty, Georgiana might have mistaken her for a servant – so plainly was she dressed.

Lydia appeared older than her years, and had a somewhat jaded look that even a spectacular poke bonnet lined in violent green and gold stripes could not hide. Her travelling gown, also of green and gold stripes, was somewhat dated in appearance. In fact Mrs Wickham was a bit of a disappointment. She was certainly a very attractive young lady, but in no way the prettiest of the Bennet sisters, as in her opinion Kitty held that position.

Lizzy noticed her lurking on the periphery of the circle and held out her hand, leaving Georgiana no option but to rejoin the noisy crowd. Surely the ladies must wish to retire to their chambers in order to remove their outer garments, gloves and bonnets? If they were to stand chattering for much longer, those without coats would become chilled.

'Georgiana, you must not be shy with my family. We are not

all as noisy as Mama and Lydia, I do assure you. Come, I shall introduce you to my father and to Mary. I am sure you will get on famously.'

Mr Bennet greeted her warmly. 'My dear Miss Darcy, I am delighted to meet you, although I must own that Kitty has told us so much about you I feel we are already acquainted.'

She dipped and returned his smile. 'We have become very close since she arrived and I shall miss her when she leaves next week to become Mrs King. Have you met her future husband, Mr Bennet?'

'I have not yet had the pleasure, Miss Darcy, but I have been assured by my Lizzy that he is the perfect match for Kitty.' He glanced at the newly restored windows. 'I gather there was an explosion here before Christmas and that these had to be replaced. I do hope nothing so bothersome is likely to occur again. I much prefer my life to be without drama and excitement.' He said this with a commendably straight face, but his eyes drifted towards his lively wife and youngest daughter.

The fact that the ghosts at Pemberley had caused the damage on their departure was a secret that was to be kept amongst those who had been present at the time. 'I can assure you, sir, nothing untoward will take place during your visit. The architect believes the event was likely caused by combustible material from the building work that was taking place at the time.'

He looked unconvinced but fortunately did not question her explanation and was then greeted by Fitzwilliam who had just arrived from a meeting with his steward. If there was one thing she disliked above any other it was being obliged to lie, even though the truth could never be revealed under any circumstances. Lizzy beckoned to her sister Mary who reluctantly moved towards them.

'Mary, let me introduce you to Georgiana. I am sure that you will become bosom bows in no time.'

Georgiana didn't curtsy, merely nodded but Mary dipped as if she felt herself an inferior. Something about the girl struck a chord deep within her. Mary would never replace Kitty in her heart, but she was going to make every effort to win her over and make her feel part of the family.

'I am so pleased to meet you at last, Mary, and I'm hoping that you can be persuaded to remain here when your parents return to Longbourn. There is so much to do and it will be more fun if I have a companion to share it with.'

Instead of looking pleased by this announcement Mary's expression became even more subdued. 'Thank you, Miss Darcy, for your kind offer of employment, but I shall return to Longbourn where I can be a comfort and help to Mama.' She turned away and walked over to join Mrs Bennet and Mrs Wickham, who were being gently ushered towards the Great Staircase by Jane.

'Oh, Lizzy, how absolutely dreadful! I have mortally offended your sister and all I wished to do was make her welcome.'

'Georgiana, my dear, Mary is often quick to take offence when none was offered. Do not worry, I shall speak to her later and explain that you are not offering to employ her as your companion but wished her to be a sister to you.'

'Is Mrs Wickham not to be introduced to me?'

'Fitzwilliam does not wish you to be intimate with her. Indeed, I am surprised that he relented and has allowed her to come to Kitty's wedding. Lydia has been warned to make no approaches to you. You will, of course, be civil to each other, but it must be no more than that.'

2

The gentlemen vanished to the billiard room and Georgiana followed Lizzy and Jane to the small drawing room. 'Lizzy, if Fitzwilliam is so set against Mrs Wickham why did he allow her to come to Pemberley?'

Her sister-in-law settled herself comfortably on a daybed before answering. 'Kitty wanted all her sisters to attend her wedding and, as he is very fond of her, he did not have the heart to refuse.'

Both Lizzy and Jane were increasing and their babies were due sometime in July. Georgiana knew little about such matters but did think it strange that Lizzy should be twice the size of Jane and already suffering from swollen ankles and other such unpleasantness. Although she thought she might be in love with Major Brownstone, she had no intention of becoming his wife in the immediate future.

Kitty had explained to her that children were an inevitable part of sharing one's bed with one's husband and, as she had no wish to fill a nursery even with someone as handsome as the major, she must remain single until she was ready to be a mama.

'Georgiana, you are wool-gathering. I asked you if you would be kind enough to find the novel I was reading earlier. I cannot remember where I last saw it.'

'Of course I will fetch it for you, Lizzy. I am certain you had it with you at luncheon. I shall go right away and look in the small dining room.' Something occurred to her as she reached the door. 'Will Adam and Major Brownstone be joining us for dinner?'

'Indeed they will – my parents have yet to meet their future son-in-law, which is unusual to say the least. As Fitzwilliam gave Adam permission to address Kitty, there was no need for him to make the long journey to Longbourn and speak to Mr Bennet.'

Jane, now seated opposite her sister in an upright padded chair, joined in the conversation. 'Papa gave his consent in writing, Lizzy, so everything is as it should be. I am quite certain he will approve of Adam. As Darcy now considers him a friend, Adam is bound to impress both of our parents.'

Georgiana still found it strange to hear Mr King addressed so informally by everyone, but it was not her prerogative to comment. She hurried on her errand, her head buzzing with possibilities. Her brother had changed since he had married Lizzy; she had softened his reserve so that he now seemed more approachable and less haughty. A year ago the only friend he had was Bingley and now he had Adam included in his inner circle. Was it possible he would ever consider Major Brownstone in the same way?

If Fitzwilliam did not approve of the major, he would not have been invited to join them tonight. It was a conundrum that she could have feelings for the major when she was certain she had no wish to marry him – no, that was not quite true – it would be fair to say she had no desire to be married to any gentleman at the moment.

Kitty had only known Adam since last December, had not even had a Season or reached her nineteenth birthday, but had absolutely no doubt at all she wished to be married. The dining room was empty and decidedly chilly now the fire had been allowed to die down. Pemberley was her home, a magnificent edifice, the biggest and most splendid establishment in the whole of Derbyshire, but its sheer size made the building impossible to keep warm. It had been far more comfortable living at the Old Rectory where Kitty would be moving to next week.

She found the book immediately. Lizzy had left it where not even a diligent servant would have seen it, for it was under the table. With the novel in her hand she began the long trek through the house to rejoin her sisters. She was just entering the central flagstone passageway that bisected the house when someone called her name.

'Miss Darcy, I beg your pardon, but I have been wandering about this vast place this age and am no nearer to finding the small drawing room.' Lydia ran towards her holding her skirt aloft to avoid tripping over – that she also showed an indecorous amount of ankle did not seem to bother her.

'Mrs Wickham, I apologise if you have become lost. You could have rung for a footman and he would have guided you to the drawing room. This is a large building, but it is laid out sensibly and I am sure you will have no difficulty finding your way in future.' She pointed down the passageway. 'You are almost there. I'm sure you would have arrived on your own volition very shortly.'

'Mama has retired to bed with a megrim, but I am sure she will be recovered in time for dinner tonight.'

Georgiana was about to point out that when she had a sick headache she was prostrate for days, but thought better of it. 'I expect the stress of the journey has unsettled her nerves. Shall we go and join Lizzy and Jane? It is far too cold to stand about chatting here.'

'I know we are not to become friends during my visit – Lizzy made that quite clear – but perhaps we can become acquaintances. I believe that we have a great deal in common.'

This was said with an open, sunny smile, but Georgiana had difficulty keeping her dismay from showing. How could Lydia be so unkind as to mention what might have happened in Brighton three years ago? She was relieved they had arrived at the small drawing room and she was not obliged to reply.

Lizzy was comfortably settled on a *chaise longue* and Jane was sitting opposite. Neither got to their feet on their arrival – for all its grandeur Pemberley was not a formal place to live. Lizzy had seen to that when she had taken the reins last September.

However, they were greeted with smiles and affection and that was more than enough. 'Come in, girls. You both look chilled to the bone. If there were fireplaces in the passageways, I would insist that they were kept burning both day and night.' Lizzy patted the end of her daybed and Georgiana was about to take this seat when Lydia sat there herself.

'Lizzy, one might suppose your baby was due in the spring and not the summer.' Lydia simpered and gestured to the quite noticeable roundness beneath her sister's gown. 'Do you think you could be mistaken with your dates?'

This outrageous comment caused a collective gasp and Lizzy sat bolt upright, swinging her feet to the floor. 'Lydia, if you wish to remain under my roof you will curb your tongue. Do I make myself quite clear?' Her voice was as cold as the passageway outside and Lydia's smug expression slipped.

'I beg your pardon, I was jesting...'

'Then your idea of what is amusing is in very poor taste.' Lizzy pointed to a chair at the far side of the room. 'I wish Georgiana to sit next to me. Kindly remove yourself and sit over there.'

Lydia flounced across the room but did not take the chair; instead she walked to the far end and pretended to be entranced by the vista.

Once she was out of earshot Jane spoke up. 'Oh dear, this does not bode well. I wish Kitty had not been so insistent Lydia must come to her wedding.'

'Marriage does not seem to have improved her; Fitzwilliam was right to be wary. We can hardly send her packing as it would upset Mama.' She shuddered. 'I do not think we would wish Mama to become upset. I well remember how she behaved when Lydia ran away – I don't think Fitzwilliam would stand for it.'

'I think that you are expecting twins, Lizzy; there can be no other explanation.' Georgiana had been thinking this for some time but had not wished to voice her opinion upon a subject of which she knew very little.

'Twins? Of course, why did I not think of that? Small wonder I am growing at such a remarkable rate.' Lizzy flopped back on the *chaise longue* as if not particularly pleased at the prospect of producing not one, but two potential heirs for the Pemberley estate.

'Fitzwilliam will be pleased, will he not? Having two babies – no, three as Jane will be residing in the east wing when it is completed – will be splendid.' Georgiana did not understand why neither of her sisters-in-law appeared to share her delight.

'I wish things were as simple as that, my dear, but producing twins is considered far more hazardous than producing a single baby,' Jane said.

Lizzy reached out and took Georgiana's hands. 'You must not look so worried, dearest girl. I am as strong as an ox and I am quite certain nothing untoward will happen to me or my babies. Mind you, this is merely speculation on my part – I could be carrying a single baby of magnificent proportions.'

'Surely Doctor Bevan will be able to examine you and confirm or deny your suspicions?'

'I shall certainly ask when he comes next month. There is no need to worry about this possibility at the moment, Georgiana. Promise me you will not mention anything to Kitty or Mama. I have no wish to upset either of them at this happy time.'

'I wish I had not mentioned it, but after Lydia...'

'Forget what she said. I already have, dearest. Now, I have no wish for Fitzwilliam to know of any of this. Will you promise me that what has taken place here will remain a secret between us until after the wedding? I am certain that he would have Lydia's bags packed within minutes if he knew.'

Although this chamber was called the small drawing room, this was really a misnomer, for there was enough space for two dozen people to sit comfortably and still be able to converse in private. Georgiana stared at the girl at the far end of the room and, for the first time in her life, understood what it was to hate someone.

* * *

'Jonathan, I have no intention of changing my mind. I knew the moment that I saw Kitty I would marry her, and I intend to do so in five days' time, with or without your approval.' Adam King glared at his friend who was unbothered by his anger.

'That is all I wanted to hear you say. As your groomsman, it is my job to ensure that you wish to tie yourself to a young lady you have only known for three months.'

'You are forgetting, my friend, that she lived under this roof until last week and that we have spent more time in each other's company than most betrothed couples do in a long engagement.'

'Remember, less than two years ago you were fighting at my side, and in that short space of time you became a man of the cloth – renounced your vows and became involved in the supernatural. Do you not think you are rushing into matrimony? Why not leave it until you have settled into being a gentleman of leisure?'

'Stow it, Brownstone, or I shall floor you.'

Jonathan chuckled. 'There is no need for fisticuffs, Adam. I give you my word as an officer and gentleman that I shall say no more on this subject. Kitty Bennet is a delightful young lady and will make you a perfect wife.' He yawned and his jaw cracked loudly. He had been staying up too late and drinking too much since he had returned to the Old Rectory three days ago.

'I thought you had a *tendre* for Georgiana and would be joining me in wedded bliss before the year is out.'

'Have I been so obvious in my regard for her? We get on well together, but she is too young to become a serving officer's wife and I have no intention of resigning my commission. The king is going to need every experienced officer to fight the French and I would be betraying my country and my regiment if I stepped aside for something as trivial as love.'

Adam frowned. 'In which case, you have behaved poorly. I have become fond of Georgiana and will not stand by and see you break her heart.'

'I think you underestimate her. She has made it very clear to me she has no wish to follow the drum and she is well aware that I intend to remain a serving officer. We agreed we should be friends, enjoy each other's company, but with no expectation of anything permanent coming from the relationship – at least at the moment.' Seeing the expression on his friend's face made him realise he had made a grave error of judgement. Showing such partiality for a young lady without making her an offer was tantamount to ruining her reputation.

'There is no need to say what you are thinking, Adam. Darcy will be expecting me to speak to him after the wedding, will he not?'

'Indeed he will, in fact everybody is expecting you to ask permission to pay your addresses to Georgiana.'

The situation was nothing short of ridiculous. Jonathan gave a snort of laughter. 'In fact the only person who will not be expecting me to do so is Georgiana herself. She wishes to have a Season in London "before she becomes entangled with a gentleman". They were her words exactly. Please excuse me. I shall pen her a note explaining the situation so that she is prepared for me to...' He was unable to finish his sentence, not sure if his friend would understand.

'Feel free to send one of my footmen with your letter. You are right to be concerned. Darcy would never have permitted you to spend so much time alone with his sister if he was not convinced you intended to make an offer for her sooner rather than later. There is one thing you do not wish to do, my friend, and that is make an enemy of Fitzwilliam Darcy.'

Having excused himself, Jonathan made his way to the study where he would find the necessary requirements for writing his note. The room was pleasantly warm and he found a fresh pen, paper and sealing wax on the desk ready for use.

He would have to assume Georgiana was allowed to receive letters without them being perused first by either her sister-in-law or her brother. What he was going to write was for her eyes only – it would be an unmitigated disaster for anyone else to read the contents.

My dear Miss Darcy,

I'm writing to warn you that your brother is expecting me to make you an offer after the wedding. I know, for we have spoken of it together, that you have as little wish as I to become betrothed at the moment.

If I do not speak to your brother he will think I have been playing fast and loose with your feelings. Therefore, for both our sakes, I am suggesting that we pretend to be betrothed. I shall speak to Darcy as if I intend to marry you in the autumn, but we will both know this to be a Banbury tale.

Our false engagement will prevent the tabbies gossiping and keep your good name intact. We have become good friends, I hope, and I would not like to lose your friendship. Although at this time neither of us wishes to embark on matrimony, I can assure you that when my duty is done things will be different. I shall resign my commission, and if you are still single, I shall be appearing at Pemberley in the hope that you will do me the honour of becoming my wife.

We can tell our families that we wish to have a long engagement, that we have no intention of marrying before the summer of next year, and this should give you ample time to break the engagement if you meet someone more to your liking.

I hold you dear to my heart,
Jonathan Brownstone, Major

He sanded the paper, folded it neatly into a square and scrawled her name on the front. He then sealed it with a blob of wax and pressed his signet ring into it. He marched to the bell strap and pulled it. When a footman appeared he was given the missive and told to deliver it immediately to Miss Darcy and not to wait for a reply.

Satisfied he had done all he could to ameliorate the situation, he strolled back to join Adam in the main drawing room. He was a soldier through and through. His milieu was the military and he found himself rather out of his depth socialising with the cream of society. The fact that his grandfather was an earl meant nothing to him. He had never met the man and his father had been estranged from him for years.

His older brother, Richard, would inherit the title and the entailed estates that went with it. He must continue to make his own way in the world. He stiffened as something appalling occurred to him. He was not in a position to make Georgiana an offer unless they were to live off her wealth.

He was not a fortune hunter and would never marry an heiress in order to better himself. Georgiana could make a match with the highest in the land – not only was she rich, she was also kind, intelligent and the most beautiful girl he had ever set eyes on.

Adam must have got things wrong – Darcy would never entertain a virtually penniless soldier as the husband for his precious sister. Dammit to hell! He must reclaim the letter before it was too late.

3

Kitty did not join the ladies in the drawing room and Georgiana had no wish to spend the remainder of the afternoon in Lydia's company so decided to go in search of her friend. 'Pray excuse me, Lizzy, Jane, I am retiring to my apartment but will rejoin you, of course, for dinner.'

Lizzy glanced at the far end of the room where Lydia was still sulking and then turned back. 'I understand, my dear. There is no need for you to remain here with us. Perhaps you could send Kitty and Mary here. I cannot remember the last time we were all together.'

'I think I can hear them coming. I was beginning to worry about their absence.' Georgiana crossed the room and opened the double doors just as the two girls arrived. Mary ignored her and walked straight across to take a chair beside Jane, but Kitty took her hands.

'Mama is asleep so we have come to join you. Are you not staying?'

'No, I have no wish to intrude on your reunion.'

'Fiddlesticks to that! I would much rather spend time with you than with Lydia or Mary.'

Georgiana choked back a laugh. 'Shush, you must not say such things. Your sisters would be deeply offended if they were to hear you speak like that. I am already at odds with Mary and I find that I cannot like Lydia at all.'

'I am not surprised, she has a natural talent for upsetting all those she comes in contact with. I cannot imagine why I wished to have her here and I sincerely regret my decision. I shall spend no more than half an hour conversing with my sisters and will then return to the apartment.'

'You had better go; Lydia is on her way over to join Lizzy and Jane.'

Georgiana slipped through the door, closing it quietly behind her. She was about to ascend the Great Stairs when there was a sudden hammering on the front door, which sent a footman racing across to open it. Curious to see who might have arrived so precipitously she paused, hoping she could catch a glimpse of who it was without being seen herself.

To her astonishment the major burst in, his shako rakishly over one eye and his dark blue military uniform liberally mud-spattered. There must be an emergency of some sort to bring him pell-mell to Pemberley. Without hesitation she stepped into view. 'Major Brownstone, has there been an accident?'

He skidded to a halt as if she was speaking in tongues. 'Accident? Why would I come here if that were the case? No, I wish to...' His voice trailed away and he ran his finger around his neck as if his stock had unaccountably tightened.

Belatedly she remembered her manners. 'Do come in, Major Brownstone. I expect you wish to speak to my brother. I shall have someone take you to the billiard room.'

'No, he is the last person I wish to speak to.' He scowled and she was certain she heard him say something very impolite under his breath.

'Whatever the reason you have arrived in such disarray, I do not think we should discuss it here. If you do not wish to see Fitzwilliam then presumably you have come to speak to me. If you would care to follow me we can converse privately in this anteroom.' She gestured towards a small chamber in which unexpected visitors were asked to wait.

She spoke to the footman who was hovering on the periphery of her vision. 'Kindly fetch refreshments for the major. Bring them to this chamber.'

Providentially, there was a merry fire burning in the grate and the room was delightfully warm after the chill of the vast vestibule. Her heart was thumping uncomfortably and an unpleasant trickle of perspiration slid between her shoulder blades. There could only be one reason why he had arrived in such a hurry, but didn't wish to speak to Fitzwilliam. He was about to break her heart.

She selected an upright chair and sat down, glad her legs had not given way beneath her. He had the good sense to leave the door open but seemed reluctant to be seated himself. He paced the floor, his expression grim, and his incivility began to annoy her.

'Please, sir, stop prowling around the room. You are giving me a headache. I am at a loss to understand what you are doing here and I insist that you explain yourself immediately.'

The sharpness of her tone had the desired effect and he halted abruptly and stared at her through narrowed eyes. Then he snatched off his hat and flung it into the fire. Instinctively she recoiled from the explosion of flames and, before she could prevent it, she was tumbling backwards in a tangle of skirts and chair legs.

If she had thought his language inappropriate before, now it made her ears burn. He was beside her in an instant, snatched her from the floor and kicked the broken chair aside. 'I am behaving like a veritable duffer. You must think me fit for Bedlam.' He gently placed her in a small armchair next to the fire.

'Major Brownstone, I cannot imagine what has caused you to behave so... so intemperately. Up until this point I had considered you a sensible man...' A large puff of evil-smelling smoke chose that moment to engulf them both and she was unable to complete her sentence.

By the time they had finished coughing several footmen had arrived, no doubt attracted by the pungent smell of the burning military hat. Her eyes were streaming and he was in no better state. He tossed her his handkerchief and snatched up a damask napkin from the tray of a startled parlourmaid.

'There is no need to be concerned, a slight mishap with the major's hat. Please leave the tray on the marquetry side table.'

'A slight mishap, my dear, is hardly how I would describe what has happened to my shako.' His eyes were brimming with laughter and he was having difficulty containing himself.

She had intended to remain stern, but his amusement was infectious and a bubble of mirth escaped; soon they were laughing and his extraordinary behaviour was temporarily forgotten. His toe-curling smile reminded her that he was an attractive man and they were more or less alone together. After all the excitement she was quite certain Peterson, the butler, would now be hovering anxiously outside the door to step in if he considered anything improper was about to take place.

'Major, can I offer you some coffee or a slice of cake?' She nodded towards the open door and he winked. This almost sent her into a second fit of giggles.

'Thank you, Miss Darcy, coffee and cake would be quite delightful.'

'There is an unpleasant draught coming through the door. Would you be so kind as to close it a little?'

He carefully moved the door so that anyone lurking outside would be hard pressed to overhear a conversation inside. When he had safely returned to his seat he picked up his coffee and drank it in one swallow.

'I had better try and explain why I incinerated my hat.' He reached across and poured himself a second cup of the aromatic brew but this time set it down beside him on an octagonal table. 'I wrote you a letter but then realised the contents were misjudged and came at a gallop to intercept the messenger. I take it you have not received a missive from me?'

This was becoming more mysterious by the minute. 'No, I have not. Surely you would have passed the groom if he left before you?'

'One would have thought so, but I came across country and he would have stayed on the lane.' He shook his head and punched his fist into his open palm. 'I am a military man renowned for my cool head and decisive actions and yet today I have behaved like the veriest greenhorn.' He stared morosely into the fire.

The silence stretched between them and she began to feel uncomfortable. 'A slice of cake, perhaps?'

He shot back in his chair as if she had slapped him. 'Why are we talking about cake? This is beyond ridiculous. Miss Darcy, I had better be frank with you or we shall be sitting here talking banalities until the wretched letter arrives.

'Adam is under the misapprehension that you are expecting

an offer from me. He is also of the opinion that Darcy approves of the match, which is why he has allowed us to spend time together. Initially I thought he might be correct and had written with a preposterous suggestion which, on further reflection, I considered was inappropriate.'

'I should like to know what is in this letter, sir, before it reaches me.'

'Before I tell you the contents, I must ask you something. You told me several times how much you are looking forward to having a Season and being presented formally to society and had no wish to form a lasting relationship with anyone – especially me. Forgive me if I misunderstood your feelings on the subject of matrimony to a serving soldier, Miss Darcy, but I thought we were in agreement that we would remain friends and nothing more.'

The bodice of her gown seemed to be slowly squeezing the air from her chest. She had indeed said exactly that, but hearing it spoken out loud made her realise how foolish she had been. 'You are quite correct – that is exactly my opinion. However, I am at a loss to know what you could have written that prompted you to arrive so precipitously.' She was relieved her voice did not reflect her unhappiness.

'When Adam said that everybody was expecting me to make you an offer, that our closeness would damage your reputation if I did not do so, I was prompted to write the letter.'

Her misery increased. He had made her an offer and then regretted it. She had no wish to marry a gentleman who offered from duty rather than love. Despite her reservations about marriage, about following the drum, she understood in that moment that she would have accepted.

She slowly replaced the delicate porcelain cup on the tray

and stood up. 'I understand perfectly, Major Brownstone. There is no need for you to mention the subject again. I thank you for your consideration, but I can assure you that you are correct in your initial assumption. The fact that our dearest friends are marrying does not mean that we are obliged to do the same.

'I too have enjoyed our companionship, but it is possible we have given my family and your friends an erroneous impression. Therefore we must consider our friendship at an end. Thank you for visiting. If you will excuse me, I must dress for dinner.'

She swept from the room and up the stairs without revealing her heartbreak. Fitzwilliam would be relieved she was not about to become embroiled in another scandal. Adam was quite wrong: her brother would never have allowed her to marry a penniless soldier.

* * *

Jonathan barely restrained his impulse to pick up the tray and hurl it across the room. He had mismanaged the situation badly and caused her unnecessary embarrassment and distress. She was quite right to dismiss him; he deserved all her opprobrium. The sooner he was back with his regiment where he could do no further harm, the happier he would be.

He wasn't sure what had happened to his unfortunate horse when he had vaulted from the saddle and charged in. Presumably one of the many stableboys had taken it and he would find his mount safely housed in a loose box.

He drained the last of the coffee and snatched up a slice of cake. Galloping about the countryside was hungry work and he intended to return via the same route he had arrived. When he reached the stable yard he was greeted by pandemonium –

grooms running from place to place and a deal of shouting going on. He waylaid a lad.

'What is amiss? Can I be of assistance?'

The boy paused. 'There's bin a right nasty accident just down the lane. Two of the carriages has overturned, and there's nags loose all over the countryside.'

Darcy should hear about this. If Pemberley was the nearest house, the injured would be brought here and his housekeeper and butler must be prepared. Instead of retracing his steps, he pounded down the path that led directly to a side entrance. He hammered on the door and got an immediate response.

Ignoring the footman he rushed past, intending to raise the alarm. He skidded to a halt on the polished floor. He had no idea in which direction to go. He turned and saw the footman close behind him.

'Take me to Mr Darcy immediately. Inform your housekeeper and butler that there has been a serious carriage accident and there will be casualties arriving. The physician must be sent for as well.'

The bewigged young man did not question his authority. 'The billiard room is at the end of this corridor, sir; the gentlemen are in there. I shall convey your message to Mr Peterson and Mrs Reynolds directly.'

Satisfied he had done everything necessary apart from inform Darcy, Jonathan strode down the length of the passageway and walked straight into the billiard room. The chamber was empty. He frowned; it was unusual for a servant not to know where his master was. Then he heard voices coming faintly from somewhere at the far end of the room and headed in that direction.

'Darcy, it is I, Major Brownstone. I wish to speak to you

urgently.' His voice, at parade-ground level, easily carried the length of the room.

There was the sound of chairs crashing over and then Darcy, with Bingley close behind, appeared. 'What the devil do you want, Brownstone? I do not take kindly to uninvited visitors yelling in my billiard room.'

'There has been a serious carriage accident and the casualties are on their way here. Three vehicles were involved. I have informed your staff, and I am now informing you.' Jonathan stopped halfway down the room and waited for the others to join him. He could see why Adam had told him that Darcy would make a formidable enemy. The man was approaching rapidly, his expression murderous.

Darcy halted at arm's length from him and if he had not been a battle-hardened soldier he might have flinched. Instead he held up a hand in a gesture of peace. 'I beg your pardon, Darcy, if I have offended you by my military manners. It is in my nature to take charge and I believe I might have overstepped my authority.'

For a moment the matter hung in the balance and then Darcy half-smiled. 'And I beg your pardon, sir, for overreacting. I shall come with you, Brownstone. Bingley, would you be kind enough to tell the ladies before joining us?'

As if from nowhere a topcoat, gloves and hat appeared and Darcy pulled them on as they thundered through the house and back to the stables. Jonathan's mount was saddled and ready, he vaulted aboard and set off after the diligence and cart he could see in the middle distance. He was certain Darcy would not be far behind.

* * *

Georgiana was, for the second time, on her way to her apartment when Bingley hurried across the entrance hall and vanished in the direction of the small drawing room. She was tempted to follow and see what had caused him to abandon his normal languid way of movement but was still too upset about her encounter with the major.

Her friend, with whom she shared an apartment, was safely ensconced with her sisters so she would have the chambers to herself. She needed to spend time alone and try and make sense of what had happened. The major was quite right to say that she had expressed on more than one occasion a desire to remain unmarried until she had at least one Season in Town. It was also true that when they had discussed his life as a serving soldier she had said such privations and danger were not to her taste.

However, these opinions had been stated before she had developed feelings for him. A young lady was obligated to appear uninterested in any eligible bachelor she met if she did not wish to be seen as hanging out for a husband. They had spent three days together before he had returned to his regiment and then she had not had any contact with him until he came back two weeks ago.

They had not corresponded whilst he had been away, but if she was honest he had been constantly in her thoughts during the intervening weeks. Indeed, even the excitement and pleasure of the Christmas festivities, the planning for Kitty's wedding and their imminent return to Pemberley, had failed to push him from her mind.

Although Fitzwilliam and Lizzy had made no mention of there being an understanding between the major and herself, they had been allowed to spend an inordinate amount of time together, some of it unchaperoned apart from the ever-present servants. Now she came to think of it, Ellie, her personal maid, had been forever coming to ask for instructions, or clarifications to instructions, when she had been sitting alone with him in the library.

There was only one thing she could do, and that was speak privately to Lizzy. No doubt there would be an opportunity sometime this evening. For now she would remain quietly in her apartment and read a book.

4

'Oh dear, I fear our pleasant afternoon is about to be interrupted, girls.' No sooner had Lizzy spoken than the door flew open and Charles burst in.

'I have come to warn you that we are about to have unexpected visitors. Brownstone was here to tell us there has been an accident nearby and they will be bringing the injured parties to Pemberley.'

Lizzy scrambled from the daybed in such a hurry that she was obliged to remain still for a moment as her head spun unpleasantly. Whilst she was recovering, Jane and Kitty were on their feet.

'You do not look at all the thing, Lizzy dearest,' Jane said. 'You must remain here and allow Kitty and I to take care of things. Do you think the apartment that you used last year will be suitable to receive those unfortunate enough to have been hurt in the accident?'

'Thank you, Jane, but I was just a little faint. I am quite well now. We shall all go and see how we can be of assistance. I am sure that Reynolds will already have matters in hand and will be preparing the downstairs rooms.' She glanced across at Lydia and was unsurprised to see her youngest sister pick up a periodical and begin to read. 'Charles, has Fitzwilliam gone to the scene?'

'Yes, he went with the major. Can't think what the fellow was doing in this direction, but he is exactly the man for a crisis. Pity Adam isn't here as well – two soldiers are better than one.' He planted a kiss on Jane's cheek. 'Good, my valet has arrived with my coat at last. I must see if I can be of any help.' He shrugged into his riding coat and dashed off down the passageway.

The three of them trooped out into the corridor and were met by the housekeeper. 'Madam, Doctor Bevan has been sent for and I am getting the apartment downstairs prepared. We have no clear notion of what has happened, or how many poor travellers are involved, but word from the stable yard is that two carriages collided and one has overturned.'

A trickle of fear ran down Lizzy's back. All the lanes and roads around Pemberley were narrow, and a coachman was obliged to sit on the box and blow his horn loudly every time they approached a bend in the road. Presumably one of the drivers had failed to do this and the vehicles had collided. Fitzwilliam had told her about a similar accident that had taken place no more than a year ago in which a horse and two passengers had been fatally injured.

'Make sure that Cook has been alerted as well, Reynolds, for I am certain refreshments will be needed. Have you had blankets fetched down from the linen cupboards?' The woman nodded. 'Do we have sufficient clean cloths to tear up for bandages?'

'Yes, madam, we do. There will also be plenty of hot water

ready by the time the victims arrive. Do you wish me to prepare guest rooms for those that are able to take the stairs?'

'I think that an excellent idea. I believe everything is in hand; Mrs Bingley and I shall wait in the entrance hall until someone arrives.'

Kitty shook her head. 'I think that you and Jane should return to the drawing room. You are both increasing and I am sure that neither of your husbands would approve of you being here. Georgiana and I are quite capable of greeting any arrivals and seeing that they are well taken care of.'

'Lizzy, I think Kitty is correct. Come along, you are already shivering, and the last thing you want to do is get a head cold.' Jane slipped her arm around her sister's waist and practically bundled her away.

* * *

Georgiana was immersed in her novel when Kitty rushed in. 'You must come downstairs at once; there has been a dreadful accident and we are to act as hostesses to the halt and the lame when they arrive. The gentlemen have gone, and the housekeeper and a bevy of servants are busy getting everything ready.'

'I shall come at once. It is decidedly chilly in the entrance hall despite having two huge fires burning day and night. A shawl is out of the question, so I think we must put on a pelisse.'

'Do you think it might not appear strange for us to greet people with our coats on?'

'I should think they will have more important things to worry about than how we are dressed. I'm going to change into my half-boots as well – slippers would not be suitable if we are obliged to go outside and offer assistance.'

Georgiana tossed her book aside and jumped to her feet.

Within a short space of time they were both suitably accoutred and on their way across the gallery and down the marble staircase.

'Have you any idea exactly where this accident took place, Kitty?'

'I have not, but I imagine it cannot be far away. Look, I can just see a slow procession turning into the drive.' Georgiana paused on the staircase and pointed through the long mullioned windows that overlooked the front of the house. 'There are two gigs, a cart and a diligence, plus several horsemen.'

She swallowed a lump in her throat. Even from this distance she could make out the distinctive, dark blue uniform of Major Brownstone. Of course, he would have been at the scene of the accident – she would expect nothing else from him – but it was going to be difficult seeing him again so soon after their distressing conversation.

'I should think it will be a further quarter of an hour before we will be needed to welcome anyone,' Georgiana said, 'so we have ample time to speak to Lizzy and see exactly what she wishes us to do.'

'I'm beginning to feel that my very presence attracts disaster. When I arrived last December dear Charles took a tumble in the carriage, which was entirely my fault. When the wretched ghosts appeared they came because of me. Now, there has been another accident. The sooner I become Mrs King and leave Pemberley, the safer you will all be.'

'Kitty, you are talking fustian; you are just overwrought because of your approaching nuptials. Bingley's accident was nobody's fault – that is why it was called an accident. Come along, we must see that everything is ready. Lizzy is relying on us.'

The weather was remarkably fine for March and the grounds were brimming with daffodils and other spring flowers. With luck, her dearest friend would have a fine day for her wedding and it would neither rain nor snow. Last March had been appalling; if she was getting married she would insist the occasion took place in the summer.

Lizzy had no further instructions for them and so they returned to wait in front of the fire in the entrance hall. 'Kitty, I am surprised that Mr Wickham does not object to his wife making a prolonged stay at Pemberley when he is not allowed to visit himself.'

'Lydia said that Wickham is staying with family friends in the neighbourhood in order to be on hand to take her home after the wedding.'

'In which case, I sincerely hope I do not have the misfortune to meet him. He is an unprincipled rogue and I wish Fitzwilliam was in the position to prevent him from coming within twenty miles of here.'

Kitty was aware that Wickham had attempted to entice Georgiana into an elopement several years ago, which was why he was *persona non grata* at Pemberley. 'Please do not distress yourself – Wickham would not dare to intrude. Lizzy has told Lydia, in no uncertain terms, that if she was to attempt to visit with him whilst she lives under this roof, she will be sent packing.'

'I'm relieved to hear you say so, dearest, and I shall not mention his name again. I think we should go out and wait in the turning circle; I believe I can hear footmen and maids gathering outside.'

Georgiana headed for the front door, which was promptly opened by a waiting footman. 'Leave the door open; there will be a deal of toing and froing once the carriages and carts arrive.'

She turned to Kitty as something else occurred to her. 'It is quite possible that there are injured servants as well. I do hope Reynolds has made suitable arrangements for them.'

She stepped into the late afternoon sunshine and, as she had expected, the cavalcade was almost upon them. Fitzwilliam rode up to her and dismounted, tossing his reins to a waiting stable boy.

'This is a damnable business, my dear. Two coachmen have broken their necks and I fear that one of the young bucks might well be fatally injured too. The young man who was driving the phaeton has broken his leg, but it is his companion who is grievously hurt. The two occupants of the third carriage are unscathed, but those in the vehicle that overturned have not fared so well and there will be cuts and bruises to attend to. Did Lizzy send you out here to greet our unfortunate guests?'

'Yes, she did. We are to take those ladies and gentlemen who do not wish to retire to a chamber to the drawing room, where refreshments are waiting. The downstairs apartment is ready to receive anyone requiring medical attention.'

The diligence and pony cart edged off to the left and disappeared towards the rear of the building. Presumably these contained the servants who had suffered some sort of damage in the accident. Georgiana hurried forward to greet the first arrivals, with Kitty close behind her.

The major had managed to organise for all four Pemberley vehicles to be harnessed and sent out on this errand of mercy. The barouche, which was approaching more slowly at the rear of the procession, appeared to have the more seriously injured – no doubt it had been easier to transport these in an open carriage.

The gig rocked to a halt first and an elderly gentleman with a florid complexion, a bald pate and frock coat descended first.

He turned to assist a stout lady of middle years, dressed in an expensive but dated travelling ensemble, to get out.

'I shall take these two inside, Kitty; will you greet the occupants of the next one?' Her friend nodded, her usual lively expression subdued. The major was riding beside the barouche looking grim.

'I am Miss Darcy, you are most welcome at Pemberley. Would you care to come inside with me where you shall be taken care of?'

The gentleman nodded. 'Trelawney's me name, and this lady's me wife. Some jackanapes travelling too fast swerved to avoid an unfortunate rider and overturned his carriage into mine. I fear the occupants of his vehicle have not been as fortunate as us.' He frowned and glanced towards the approaching carriages. 'We are on our way to visit my daughter who has just produced our first grandson; she will be expecting us.'

'If you would care to give their direction to one of my footmen, a message will be conveyed immediately. He will reassure your family that you are unhurt and will be overnighting at Pemberley and shall continue your journey in one of our carriages tomorrow.'

She led the way into the entrance hall and gestured towards the marble stairs where Reynolds was waiting with a group of servants. 'We have chambers prepared and the housekeeper has maids waiting if you require their help.' Georgiana smiled encouragingly. 'As soon as you are feeling more the thing you will be escorted to the drawing room where refreshments will be waiting.'

He turned to his wife. 'I've no need to go, me dear, but will come with you if you wish.'

The lady was staring around, her eyes wide. 'Thank you, I would like the opportunity to refresh myself before joining you.'

She patted her husband's arm affectionately. 'You run along; I'll not be very long.'

At once Reynolds stepped forward and curtsied briefly. 'My girls will take you to your rooms, madam, and your luggage will be brought up to you directly it arrives.'

'We have no luggage, but I am sure we can manage for one night,' Mrs Trelawney said cheerfully.

Georgiana turned to Mr Trelawney. 'If you would care to come with me, sir, I shall take you to the drawing room. This is a large establishment and I do apologise for the lack of heat in the passageways and corridors. It is quite impossible to keep the place warm, however many fires we light.'

'A right grand place, Miss Darcy. I've never seen the like. Pemberley is mentioned in guidebooks but I never thought I'd be able to see inside meself.'

'Forgive me for asking, sir, but was anyone travelling with you injured in the accident?'

'Me coachman took a tumble from the box, but me under-coachman was unhurt and I left him taking care of me horses. Our baggage, me man and Mrs Trelawney's maid travelled ahead. Waste of time to fetch it back; we'll be on our way first thing in the morning.'

Georgiana did not like to tell this pleasant gentleman that his coachmen might very well be dead. 'Here we are. If you require anything further, do not hesitate to ask one of the footmen in attendance.'

They had now arrived outside the double doors of the drawing room – these stood open and the welcome smell of freshly baked bread, vegetable soup and meat pasties wafted towards them. The room had been transformed from a formal seating area to a chamber she scarcely recognised. From somewhere tables had been fetched and set out to the right of the door, with crisp, white tablecloths and chairs placed around them. These occupied a third of the space. Against the panelling a buffet table had been laid out with a veritable feast.

The sofas, daybeds and padded armchairs had been moved and regrouped to the left of the doors, leaving a substantial area in the centre of the room free for those who wished to remain on their feet and walk about. She was not sure how many guests were expected, but provision had been made for a dozen or more.

Cook would be waiting to hear how many extra guests there would be for dinner tonight. Kitty had said that Adam's brother, his wife and three ancient aunts were expected. Perhaps Mr Trelawney would know.

'Mr Trelawney, apart from Mrs Trelawney and yourself, do you know how many other guests we might expect to stay with us tonight?'

'A phaeton holds only two, but both the driver and his passenger was seriously injured. Silly young fool, what was he thinking of to be dashing about the countryside at such a speed?' He cleared his throat and delved into his pocket to remove his handkerchief. Georgiana waited politely until he had blown his nose and wiped his eyes.

'The other carriage, not ours you understand, tipped over, but I don't think anyone was seriously hurt. I believe there was five travellers inside, plus two on the box and a couple of outriders. I'm afraid I didn't see the occupants, so can't tell you any more.'

'If you would excuse me, Mr Trelawney, I must see if I can be of assistance elsewhere.'

'You run along, Miss Darcy; there's a fine spread here and I can help meself.'

Georgiana had a sinking feeling in the pit of her stomach.

She picked up her skirts and ran through the house to arrive just as Kitty was ushering inside those that had been travelling in the other carriage.

She breathed a sigh of relief. Whoever these people were they did not fit the description of Adam's relatives. There were three ladies and two gentlemen and none of them were elderly.

Kitty had her arm around the waist of a young lady. 'Miss Garfield has broken her arm, Mrs Garfield has cut her head and will require sutures, and I shall take them at once to see Doctor Bevan. However, the remainder of their party has emerged unscathed from their nasty experience.' Kitty guided the two patients across the vestibule, leaving her to deal with the remainder of the group.

'I am Miss Darcy. Welcome to Pemberley. There are rooms ready for you upstairs if you would care to retire. We have refreshments waiting in the drawing room, or a tray can be sent up to you – whatever you prefer.'

'I am Garfield. We were on our way to visit my brother-in-law, Sir Matthew Rawlings, who lives in the next village. This is my younger daughter, Miss Emily, and this is my son George.' The girl curtsied and the young man bowed. 'Do you want to go upstairs, Emily, or come with George and I?'

'I should like to go upstairs first, Papa, but I shall come down directly.'

The girl trotted off with a maid, exclaiming and commenting in excitement at everything she saw. Georgiana hid her smile. Miss Emily could not be above sixteen years of age and one could not expect her to view such magnificence in silence as her father and older brother were.

'If you would care to come with me, Mr Garfield, there is another traveller already in the drawing room – Mr Trelawney – and he will keep you company.'

'This is a wretched business indeed, Miss Darcy. I have lost an excellent horse and my carriage is beyond repair. They both cost me a pretty penny, I can tell you.'

Georgiana thought that the fatalities and injuries to the passengers might be considered of more importance than the expense involved, but she held her tongue.

5

By the time the unexpected guests had been catered for, refreshments had been eaten and rooms allocated, it was quite dark. Georgiana and Kitty had returned to their apartment in order to remove their outer garments and change into house slippers. Everyone had been deeply shocked to discover that not one but two human lives had been lost and three horses had had to be shot.

The major and Adam were sitting with the family in the small drawing room, the more formal chamber had been given over to the travellers. There were now seven extra to be seated at dinner as both Mrs Garfield and her daughter declared themselves well enough to join them.

'There is no point in changing for dinner tonight,' Lizzy announced. 'None of our visitors can do so. I have told Cook to serve at seven o'clock, very late I know, but I doubt that either the Garfields or the Trelawneys will be hungry before then.'

The major had been sitting at the far side of the room with the other gentlemen so Georgiana was fairly sure nobody had noticed they were avoiding each other's company. 'I am going to see if your guests require anything further, Lizzy.'

'Thank you, dearest Georgiana, I am easily fatigued at the moment and am relishing these hours spent in idleness.'

Every sconce was lit and the house, for once, felt warm and welcoming. She feared she could never feel quite the same about Pemberley, even though the ghosts had gone. The drawing room was empty – no doubt everybody had returned to their chambers to prepare for the evening. Although nobody was to dress, everyone would wish to appear at their best.

She was about to return when Peterson hurried up to her holding a silver salver balanced on one gloved hand. 'Miss Darcy, there is a letter for you. I have no idea from whence it came or for how long it has been waiting to be delivered.'

Georgiana took the missive and turned it over, but there was no indication on the outside of the carefully folded paper as to the identity of the sender and she did not recognise the scrawled hand. 'Thank you, Peterson, I am sure it is nothing urgent.'

She waited until he had retreated and then moved under the flickering yellow light of a sconce. She scratched open the blob of sealing wax. Good heavens! This was the letter the major had tried to prevent from falling into her hands. She read to the end with growing astonishment. Small wonder he had been desperate to retrieve the note before it reached her – he was quite preposterous to suggest they formed a deceitful engagement.

Then, as she considered the matter, she began to believe there was merit in his idea. Kitty had said the same, that Fitzwilliam and Lizzy had only allowed her so much leeway because they thought her feelings were engaged. However unsuitable Major Brownstone might be, they had obviously decided they would support her choice.

She must talk to the major immediately – this letter changed everything. Although he had said their engagement would be false initially, he had also written that he would return to ask her for her hand when he had completed his duty as a soldier. Fortuitously, war with France had been suspended at the Treaty of Amiens, which, no doubt, was why the major was allowed so much furlough.

There was still half an hour until everyone gathered in the Great Hall for sherry wine before dinner. That surely must be time enough to inveigle the major to speak to her in private? The small drawing room was as she had left it, Fitzwilliam, Bingley, Adam and the major at one end and Lizzy and her sisters at the other. The gentlemen must be avoiding the flummery of female conversation.

Instead of joining the other ladies, Georgiana deliberately knocked into a table sending a pile of books crashing to the floor. This drew the attention of the gentlemen and when she was certain the major was looking at her directly, she unfolded her hand and showed him the letter hidden there. Then she apologised prettily for the fuss and quickly restored the books to their allotted place.

'Lizzy, your guests have all gone upstairs. I am going to check the dining room has been correctly laid for dinner.' She did not wait for any comments but slipped away in the hope that the major would follow.

* * *

Jonathan cursed inwardly and then hastily made his excuses. 'Forgive me, gentlemen, an urgent call of nature.'

Darcy raised an eyebrow and glanced pointedly towards the door through which his sister had so recently left, but he remained quiet and Jonathan was able to escape without being cross-examined as to his motives. He was damn sure there would be a reckoning with that formidable gentleman very soon and he was not looking forward to it.

He had no need to search for Georgiana, as she was waiting at the far end of the passageway and beckoned him into one of the dozens of rooms that branched from the central corridor. He increased his pace, not wishing to be away any longer than he had to.

He strode into the small chamber and scanned her features, trying to decide if she was in a fulminating mood or more cordial. To his surprise she smiled and beckoned him in conspiratorially.

'Major Brownstone, I was quite stunned by the contents of your letter.' She raised a hand as he was about to interrupt. 'Not at your extraordinary suggestion that we pretend to be betrothed, but the fact that you said your feelings are engaged and that you have every intention of making me an offer when you are free to do so.'

He was flummoxed by her statement and scarcely knew what to reply. He could not remember the last time he had been at a loss for words. 'Miss Darcy, I meant every word of it. If the situation were different I would be down on one knee at this very moment, asking for your hand in marriage.' From deep within him his true feelings burst forth. 'Although we have been acquainted only a short time, I have fallen irrevocably in love with you.' This time it was his turn to stop *her* speaking. 'It will not do, my love; even if I were to resign my commission I would still not be in a position to make you my wife. I have only my prize money invested in the funds and no estate of my own. My pedigree is as impeccable as your own, but you are a wealthy and beautiful young heiress and must marry someone in a similar position.'

'Are you telling me that the only reason you do not wish to marry me is because I am rich and you are not?' She sounded more amused than anything else.

'You can do better than me. I am a rough soldier, for all my good breeding, and you deserve a true gentleman, one who has money and estates and can look after you properly.'

'If my brother and Lizzy consider you a suitable husband, then who are you to cavil? You would not be the first impecunious gentleman to marry a rich wife. Indeed, I understand it is quite commonplace in the *ton*.' She could not disguise the tremor in her voice and her eyes glittered with unshed tears.

He could not bear to see her distressed and forgot his determination to sever the connection for her sake, not his. He closed the gap between them and was about to embrace her when something stopped him. Doing so would obligate him to marry her, and he was certain she could do better.

Then she made the decision for him and took the final step so she was in his arms. He pressed her close to his heart, loving the feel of her softness against his chest. With a sigh of acceptance, he rested his chin on top of her head and gently stroked her back.

She tilted her face expectantly but he would resist the temptation to kiss her. That would be the outside of enough. He was breaking all the rules of etiquette by merely holding her. 'Sweetheart, this will not do, you know. We must not believe the romantic nonsense that says "love conquers all"; it would be madness on your part to tie yourself to me.'

Reluctantly he released his hold and stepped away, relieved that she did not follow him. One might have expected her to look forlorn, but she smiled so sweetly his heart turned over.

'I have decided that I wish to marry you and I will not take no for an answer. I am quite prepared to wait until you are no longer a serving soldier. I think we should become engaged as soon as the wedding is over. It is perfectly proper to have a long engagement in our circumstances. I have more than enough in my trust fund to buy a sizeable estate – you might be poor today, but once we are married my money will be yours.'

He ached to kiss her, to agree to her suggestion, but somehow he managed to remain calm. 'I shall speak to Darcy and if he agrees to your extraordinary suggestion, then I shall propose to you in style. However, you must promise me, Georgiana, that if he refuses you will accept his decision and forget about me. I am sure you will meet a fine young man in London in the coming months and will be profoundly grateful that you have not become entangled with me.'

She nodded. 'That is an excellent notion. I give you my word that I will relinquish all hope of becoming your wife if Fitzwilliam is against the match.'

The adorable minx was being far too sanguine about the matter; she was plotting some devilment that would be his undoing, of that he was sure. She handed him the letter. 'You had better take this; it would not do for anyone else to read it. Now, we have dallied here long enough and I must rejoin the others in the drawing room.'

She spun, sending her skirts in a swirl around her ankles, revealing that her silk slippers exactly matched the russet of her gown. Not waiting for him to follow she danced away as if she was the happiest girl in the world and not about to suffer from a broken heart.

He had better speak to Darcy right away. Was he being disingenuous to believe this muddle could be settled without his being pitched unceremoniously from the house for causing aspersions to be cast upon her unassailable purity?

* * *

Lizzy beckoned to her husband and moved away from Jane, Lydia and Kitty to join him at a small arrangement of furniture equidistant from the two groups. Here they should be able to converse without being overheard.

'What is it, my darling? Are you unwell? You look rather pallid and I will not have you overtaxing yourself just because we have extra visitors.' Fitzwilliam ignored the damask-covered armchair and joined her on the love seat.

'My love, what have you decided about the major and Georgiana? I know we agreed to let her infatuation run its course, but I am afraid she has formed a genuine affection for him. How is it that both Kitty and Georgiana have managed to fall in love so quickly when it took us a year to decide we were suited?'

He took her hand and gently stroked the knuckles. 'I think that what transpired here in December pushed them together. I was not surprised that Kitty fell headlong into love so quickly; she has a more lively personality than my sister. However, I must own I am at a loss to understand how Georgiana has come to do the same.'

'She imagined herself in love with Wickham all those years ago and was fortunate not to lose her reputation to that scoundrel. I believe Georgiana is more volatile than either of us realised, and now we are stuck with the consequences.'

'Consequences? Devil take it! Are you suggesting that things have progressed beyond the point of retreat? That Brownstone has made her an offer?'

For a moment she feared he would leap to his feet in order to challenge the unfortunate major to a duel. Fitzwilliam's expression was ominous – after the near disaster of the ghosts he would not tolerate a scandal at Pemberley.

'My love, if he has, then we should be pleased, not incensed – after all, he could not have done so if we had not allowed them to spend time together in the hope that Georgiana's interest would wane on further acquaintance with Major Brownstone.'

His fingers relaxed beneath hers and the danger was over. 'Lizzy, what in God's name am I to do? Should I agree to let the major become betrothed to my sister or should I forbid it?'

'You can hardly refuse your permission, my dear; that would look very odd of you. Perhaps allowing them to become engaged would not be so very bad, for Georgiana could not possibly marry him unless he resigned his commission and I'm certain he is unlikely to do that at the moment. Therefore, the betrothal would by necessity be prolonged and Georgiana will meet someone more suitable in London—'

His fingers closed painfully over her knuckles again. 'About that, I have decided to cancel her Season, with both you and Jane in an interesting condition we cannot be in London next month.'

'I rather thought you might say that, and I have already set other plans in motion. I have spoken to Adam and he is quite happy to squire Kitty and Georgiana to the soirées, balls and routs. He has promised to keep a close eye on your sister and make sure she's not importuned by any unsuitable young men.'

'I suppose that will suffice. King is a sound fellow and will keep her safe. What about the ball we had planned to hold in Grosvenor Square?'

'That must go ahead as we have already sent out invitations.

You must go. I shall be perfectly safe here without you.' She hesitated, wondering if she should share her suspicions. 'I think, my love, it is possible that we are expecting twins. If that is the case then I am likely to be delivered early, but not in April. As long as you are here from the end of May then I shall be content.'

If she had expected him to be shocked by her news she was disappointed, for he merely smiled knowingly. 'I had surmised the same, sweetheart; there could be no other explanation. I have sent for a specialist physician to attend here after the wedding. If he agrees that it will be in order for me to leave you for a week or two, then I shall go. It would be a shame if I didn't lead my sister out at her first ball.'

A footman approached, but hovered a discreet distance away until beckoned forward by Fitzwilliam. 'Major Brownstone would like to see you, sir, in the library.' The man bowed and backed away as if in the presence of royalty.

'Are you coming with me, Lizzy? I should dearly like you to. I fear I might say something I regret if you're not there to restrain my temper.'

'I think that an excellent notion. Kindly give me your arm so that I may regain my feet with a modicum of dignity. There is barely half an hour before we must gather in the Great Hall for sherry with our guests, so this had better be a brief meeting.' However, when she attempted to get to her feet, a wave of dizziness caused her to sway alarmingly.

'Sit down, darling. I shall deal with this matter myself and you must remain here.'

She did not protest; it would be foolish to traipse around the house when she was feeling so unsteady. He strode away, his shoulders rigid. She had a dreadful feeling this would not be a cordial exchange between the major and her husband.

* * *

Georgiana wasn't sure whether to return to her apartment or rejoin the party in the small drawing room. Would her agitation be obvious to her family? She had no wish to be subjected to an intrusive interrogation even by her dearest sister. She would go into the library until it was time for dinner.

A parcel of books had arrived from Hatchards the other day and she was almost certain there was a title amongst them that would suit her very well. All new acquisitions were placed on the Chinese lacquered table at the far end of the room, so she headed in that direction. Both fires were lit and the room was delightfully warm after the chilly corridors.

When she had the desired book in her hand, she decided to curl up in a high-backed, winged armchair that was already positioned away from the draughts and near enough to the grate to be comfortable. She carefully smoothed out the skirt of her gown before she sat, for she had no wish to have creases in it when she joined everyone for dinner. She had barely got settled when she heard heavy footsteps approaching and someone strode in.

Moments later a second person arrived and it was too late for her to reveal herself. Her heart was hammering, her stomach lurched. This was a conversation she had no wish to overhear.

'Well, Brownstone, what is it you wish to say to me?' Her brother sounded terse and unaccommodating. In this mood he was bound to refuse his permission and possibly call the major out for his temerity.

6

Georgiana cowered in her chair, bitterly regretting that she did not identify herself immediately. It was far too late to announce herself, so she had better remain silent until the interview was completed.

'Darcy, I am quite certain you know why I wish to speak to you. After all, have you not allowed me to spend time with your sister over the past week? You would not have done so if you had not already approved my suit.'

She held her breath. This was hardly the conciliatory approach she had expected the major to take. Fitzwilliam was bound to take umbrage at his tone and would respond in kind. To her surprise her brother remained silent, and Major Brownstone was obliged to speak again without having received an answer to his first remark.

'However, things are not exactly as you might suppose. I love Georgiana and she loves me, and one day I would dearly like to marry her, but we have decided now is not the right time. I cannot in all conscience resign my commission with the war in

France about to recommence and I have no intention of asking your sister to follow the drum – far too dangerous.'

'What exactly are you proposing, sir?'

This was spoken softly, but Georgiana knew her brother was enraged. She braced herself for a diatribe. This was going to end badly if she did not intervene. She was about to appear like a genie from a bottle when the major spoke again.

'I'm proposing that we become betrothed, then Georgiana can have her time in Town without being pestered by fortune hunters. However, if at any time she meets a young man who is more acceptable to both herself and you, then she is at liberty to break the engagement.'

'I see. An extended engagement that will satisfy the tabbies but still allow my sister a Season?' Fitzwilliam appeared pleased with this suggestion. 'An excellent compromise, major, and I give you my wholehearted support and approval. I have no wish to stop Georgiana from marrying whoever she wishes, but will be relieved if she becomes bored with the arrangement before you are in a position to marry her.'

Instead of being offended by this remark the major laughed. 'Then we are in complete accord, Darcy. Much as I love your sister, I'm well aware of my shortcomings and would wish her to find someone from her own strata of society.'

Georgiana could remain hidden no longer. She tumbled from her chair and erupted into the conversation. Fitzwilliam staggered back a step or two but the major winked at her. Good grief! The wretched man had known she was there all the time and had been saying things deliberately to provoke her.

'Major Brownstone, you are the grandson of an earl, the fact that you are impecunious is of no matter.' Then her tongue ran away with her and she said something she had not intended. 'Fitzwilliam, you have given us permission to become betrothed and you cannot retract that. However, I have decided we shall be married in June – or whenever my future husband can get furlough.' She glared at both of them, but reserved a sweet smile for the major. 'I shall accompany you until... until I am increasing and then I shall return home.'

'Well said, my love. We have been roundly hoisted by our own petards. Why wait until June? Surely we could have a double wedding with Kitty the day after tomorrow?'

Georgiana had never stamped her foot in her life but was sorely tempted to do so now. 'You are being ridiculous, and I do not take kindly to your miserable attempt at humour.' She was unabashed by her brother's expression. 'Fitzwilliam, I apologise for eavesdropping on a conversation that was not meant for me to hear, but I am glad that I did in view of what transpired. I shall now consider myself formally engaged to Major Brownstone and I expect you to announce it at dinner tonight.'

Her stomach flipped and she wished the words unsaid. Never before had she spoken to her brother so impertinently and was appalled that she had also issued him with an ultimatum. Then the major was beside her and his arm was firmly around her waist.

'This interview has been a trifle unorthodox, Darcy, but I think we all know where we stand. I shall be your brother-in-law at some point. Do not poker up, sweetheart. I give you my word you shall have your summer wedding if I am at liberty.' He ignored Fitzwilliam and turned her to face him before saying earnestly, 'You do realise, don't you, that you will have to remain at Pemberley, as I have no estate in which you can live?'

'I would prefer to remain here. Jane and Bingley will be moving into the east wing as soon as the renovations are completed, and this place is so vast I could remain here even if we had a dozen children, and no one would be any the wiser.' Her brother's sudden bark of laughter startled her.

'Georgiana, you are incorrigible. Six months ago you would not have spoken to me so fiercely, but I am pleased that you did. Now I know that you are a woman grown and quite able to take charge of your own destiny. I hope you will reconsider your wish to traipse all over the continent with Brownstone, but if you do decide that is your desire, then I shall do all that I can to make your travels easier.'

The major pushed her gently towards Fitzwilliam and she left the shelter of her beloved's arms and rushed to embrace her brother. 'There is no need to do anything precipitous. On consideration I think it would be unfair to announce anything until after the wedding. This week is Kitty's time to celebrate; I am quite content to wait before you make the announcement.' Belatedly she realised she should have asked the major what he thought, but it was too late to retract; the words were already spoken.

'I shall leave you and Brownstone alone to discuss what has happened. I promise I shall tell no one apart from Lizzy.' His arms closed around her a second time and he kissed her on top of her head, and then he strode away, apparently unbothered that she had just become betrothed to a penniless soldier.

'Are you going to remain standing, my dear, or do you prefer to be seated?'

'Why should I wish to sit down, sir?'

'And another thing, sweetheart, I insist that from now on you use my given name. After all, do you ladies not all refer to my friend as Adam?'

'Very well, Jonathan, by some extraordinary happenstance we find ourselves betrothed.'

'You are quite ridiculous, my darling, and I believe that

married to you I shall be run ragged. Now, are you ready?' He bowed deeply and dropped to one knee. 'Miss Georgiana Darcy, will you do me the inestimable honour of becoming my wife? Please make me the happiest of men, as I am like to fade away from a broken heart if you do not accept my offer.'

Instead of replying she raised her foot and placed it on his chest, giving him a none-too-gentle shove. He lost his balance and tumbled backwards. She scarcely had time to laugh at his predicament before his arm shot out and grasped her ankle, sweeping her feet from under her. She landed with a painful thud on her derriere and all desire to laugh vanished.

'That was quite uncalled for: a gentleman would not have just done as you did.' She attempted to regain her feet but became entangled in her skirts. With one smooth motion he sprung up and then reached down and brought her up beside him.

'I love you to distraction, sweetheart, but I fear that this betrothal is going to be tempestuous.' He cupped her face and dropped a feather-light kiss on her lips. 'You do realise that you have not answered my proposal.'

Her mouth was still tingling from the contact with his. 'Of course I will marry you, but I'm not sure that I wish to do so this summer – perhaps the following year would be more suitable?'

'I am yours to command, Miss Darcy, and am resigned to stepping into parson's mousetrap whenever you wish.'

She giggled. These were hardly the words of a man overwhelmed by love. 'When you take my commands, Major Brownstone, I shall sprout wings and fly. Now, I believe that I just heard the dinner gong, so we must repair to the Great Hall and mingle with our guests. As far as everyone else is concerned, we are no more than casual acquaintances.'

He brushed off his breeches and smiled ruefully. 'I shudder

to think what damage you might inflict on me if we were *actually* betrothed.'

Now he was being deliberately annoying. 'We *are* betrothed as you well know, and if you continue to behave in this vein I shall not be answerable for the consequences.'

He tucked her waving hand under his arm and smiled down at her like an elderly, benevolent uncle. 'I had no idea you were such a volatile young lady, Miss Darcy. I'm not sure that a man of my decrepitude...'

This was too much. She had no idea why he was deliberately acting the fool, but it was quite intolerable. She snatched her hand away and kicked him hard in the shins. She regretted this rash action as her soft silk slippers were no match for his polished Hessians.

He waited, his expression bland, the picture of polite attentiveness, whilst she hopped about the passageway clutching her injured toes. There was something about this gentleman that made her behave irrationally when she was renowned for her quiet and calm demeanour.

'If you have quite recovered, my dear, I believe I can hear people approaching.'

Immediately she straightened, shook out her skirts and gave him her most disdainful look. His eyes were brimming with amusement and she was tempted to attack him for a second time, but thought better of it. Instead she stalked off and his vexing laughter followed her down the flagstone passageway.

The family and their unexpected guests, even those that had been injured, were gathered in the Great Hall. She was tardy and expected her brother to treat her to one of his disapproving stares. However, he merely smiled and returned to his conversation with Mr Trelawney.

As expected the ladies had congregated in one fluttering

circle and the gentlemen in another. For some reason this always happened before dinner, but when the gentlemen abandoned their port, the two groups mingled. She drifted up and spoke quietly to her sister-in-law.

'I do apologise for not being here sooner, Lizzy. Is there anything you wish me to do?'

'You are not at all late, Georgiana. Jane and I have only just arrived. Now, let me introduce you again to our guests. This is Mrs Garfield and this is her eldest daughter, Miss Garfield. I believe you have already met Miss Emily.'

Georgiana curtsied politely and the two young ladies returned the compliment but said nothing. Their mother merely nodded and she was surprised at this frosty reception.

'Take the girls on a short tour of the downstairs rooms, Georgiana, and Mrs Garfield and I will remain here and have a cosy chat.'

'I should be delighted to show you around. It will have to be brief as we will be called in to dinner shortly.' As soon as they were out of earshot Miss Garfield touched her arm.

'I do apologise for my mother's rudeness, Miss Darcy. She had great hopes that I would make a match with my second cousin, Sir Matthew's son, but Lady Rawlings seems set on marrying him to you.'

'Good heavens! I cannot think where she got that extraordinary notion from. Mr Rawlings and I have never been more than acquaintances, occasional dance partners, and I have never looked on him in that way. Indeed, I have just become betrothed to Major Brownstone and we are to be married in the summer.'

If she had announced that she was about to tread the boards she could not have received a more shocked reception. She wished her words unsaid. Had they not decided to keep the matter secret until after the wedding? Now it was too late – she prayed her indiscretion was not going to cause her dearest friend any upset.

Miss Emily giggled nervously. 'Oh dear, I beg you do not mention this to Mama. She will force Estelle to marry our cousin before he sets his cap at someone else.'

'I should not have mentioned it at all, for we are not announcing it until after Miss Bennet is married to Mr King the day after tomorrow. I can assure you nothing will be said at dinner and I would be immensely grateful if you would keep this knowledge to yourselves until my brother makes the engagement official.'

Miss Garfield nodded vigorously. 'We shall forget we ever heard the news. Whilst Cousin Peter believes he is a contender for your hand, he will not look in my direction. I have no wish to speak ill of him, but I cannot like him. He has an unsavoury reputation. Papa is not happy with my mother's choice, but he will go along with it, as he does with everything else she decides.'

This comment had piqued Georgiana's interest. She thought Mr Rawlings rather wild, but had not considered him unsavoury – whatever that might mean. 'He was involved in an incident here last year with his cronies, but it was no more than high spirits. He has always been perfectly pleasant to me and I have not heard anything untoward about him. What has he done to earn your opprobrium?'

The two girls exchanged knowing glances and then drew her into the shadow of a large marble bust. 'I heard Papa tell Mama that he was "a rackety fellow" and that "this young man spends too much time in dens of iniquity". I am almost certain that means he would not make a suitable match for me.' Miss Garfield plucked at her fashionable skirt. 'I have a large dowry and I'm sure I could find someone more to my liking if I was to be allowed a London Season.'

'I am to have one even though I shall already be engaged. If you give me your address in Town, I shall make sure you and your family are invited to my ball and that you have introductions to all the eligible young men.'

There was no time for further conversation as a footman appeared and banged the gong loudly. She escorted her new friends through the vestibule, across the Great Hall, and they were able to join the end of the line without their absence being noted.

There were no designated places apart from those for Lizzy and Fitzwilliam at the head of the table. It would have been more usual for the hostess to sit at the far end, opposite her spouse, but her brother had refused to continue this custom. He had said he had no intention of shouting down the table at his wife when he could have her sitting next to him.

'Look, there are three seats together on the right. Shall we go there? If you, Miss Garfield, sit between your sister and I, then we can help you. Is your arm very sore? I am surprised that Doctor Bevan allowed somebody with a broken arm to wander about the place as you are doing.'

'My arm is not broken, thank the Lord, merely badly sprained. He assured us I should be perfectly well in a few days.' Miss Garfield nodded towards her mother who was seated next to Jane. 'Mama was also fortunate as she only required three sutures and these have been disguised by her turban.'

'The young gentleman and his companion who caused the accident have not been so lucky. One of them will never walk again and the other remains unconscious. Two coachmen were fatally injured.' Miss Emily dabbed her eyes on her napkin.

'It is a truly dreadful thing to have happened, Emily.

However, we must pray that both of the young men make a full recovery. I am certain that provision will be made for the families of the men who died. Now, look at all the delicious treats that have been placed on the table. I cannot remember seeing such a spread before.' Miss Garfield waved her uninjured arm and her sister immediately forgot her distress and began exclaiming over the various dishes.

Georgiana wished she had not been so eager to sit with these two girls. She hoped no one in her family had dismissed the tragedy of the two servants so casually. The meal progressed and as more wine was consumed the talk became noisier. Cook had excelled herself. Each course had several removes and all were as good as the other. However, she was relieved when eventually Lizzy put down her napkin and pushed herself to her feet.

Lydia was talking gaily to both Adam and Jonathan, but Mrs Bennet was remarkably subdued, not a bit like the garrulous woman she had met earlier. Mary was barely visible at the far end of the table and she had no idea how she was reacting to the splendour of a Pemberley dinner.

'Come along, we must go now and leave the men to their port.' Georgiana had been surprised to see that both girls had accepted a glass or two of wine and were now even more lively than before. She rather feared she would be obliged to remain with the Garfield girls for the remainder of the evening.

She took the elbow of each and guided them through the double doors, down the wide central passageway and into the music room and then pushed them gently in the direction of a daybed. 'If you would care to sit here, I am going to play the pianoforte. Mrs Darcy and Mrs Bingley prefer to sit quietly until the gentlemen come in.'

Before they could protest at her abandonment, she hurried to the far end of the vast room where the musical instruments were kept. Kitty had been sitting with her future husband during dinner and Georgiana had had no time to talk to her.

'Shall we play a duet? I think the Garfield sisters are a little overcome by alcohol. I dread what they might do or say next.'

'We are about to find out, dearest, for they are charging in our direction.'

7

'Miss Darcy, Miss Bennet, my sister plays the harp and I am said to have a beautiful singing voice. Shall we entertain together?' Miss Garfield was a trifle unsteady. 'It is fortunate that our talents are so arranged, as I would have great difficulty playing a harp with only one arm available.' She nodded sagely and Georgiana busied herself at the pianoforte in order to hide her smile.

Kitty came to her rescue. 'I suggest that you and Miss Emily take the lead. Miss Darcy and I shall accompany if we know the piece you play.'

Whilst the two girls tottered about making themselves ready Georgiana whispered to her friend, 'We must pray that the gentlemen remain in the dining room until they have completed their performance. I blame myself for their inebriation; I should not have allowed the footmen to replenish their glasses so frequently.'

'Fiddlesticks to that! They are old enough to know better and their behaviour is not your concern. Do you think we should warn the others?'

Georgiana glanced down the enormous chamber. 'They are

all sitting at the far end by the fire and I doubt they will be disturbed by the music. I am surprised that Lydia and Mary have not joined us but remain with the older ladies.'

Miss Garfield called across to them, 'We are ready; we are going to perform "Greensleeves". I am certain that you must have the music somewhere if you do not know it already.'

'I know it. Kitty, do you?' When her friend nodded, Georgiana made room on the wide piano stool. 'If we play with sufficient energy, we might be able to drown out the harp and singing.'

'It might not be as bad as you fear. They both look steadier than they did a quarter of an hour ago.'

Before either of them had time to draw breath, the Garfield girls launched into their version of 'Greensleeves'. Georgiana doubted that even when perfectly well Miss Emily could play a harp proficiently, and if her sister's voice was considered good, then she was glad she was not obliged to attend a musicale in their neighbourhood.

After a few minutes, Kitty was laughing so hard she could not continue. The speed at which this traditional folk song was being performed rendered it impossible to keep pace on the piano. 'Shall we leave them to it? I am sure they will not notice that we have abandoned them.' Georgiana quietly closed the instrument, and she and Kitty slid from the stool and tiptoed away.

Once they were ten yards from the caterwauling and hideous plunking they paused. 'They should have completed the song in ample time. Look, Kitty, the rest of the party are transfixed. We had better join them. We must be careful what we say, as their mama might take exception if we criticise their performance.'

* * *

Jonathan had no desire to sit drinking port in the dining room. Georgiana had been studiously ignoring him, but he was determined to spend the remainder of the evening in her company. Whatever her feelings on the subject, Darcy had given them permission to marry in the summer and would think it odd if his sister was not talking to her future husband.

The port was on its second journey round the table when he was sure he heard the sound of cats fighting. He ignored the decanter and pushed it straight on to Garfield who was on his right. What the devil was that hideous screeching sound?

Nobody else appeared to have heard anything, but he was determined to investigate. After the terrifying incident with the ghosts last December, anything untoward should be explored. He pushed his chair back and nodded at Darcy. 'Can you hear that noise? Sounds like animals in agony. I'm going to find out what it is.'

He now had the company's full attention and the table fell silent as all strained to hear. Darcy slapped his hand on the table and laughed out loud. 'Not animals, Brownstone, but a human singer and possibly a harpist. Come, this is too good to miss. We shall join the ladies and enjoy the entertainment.'

Garfield seemed reluctant to accompany them. 'That will be my girls; I could recognise that sound anywhere. Mrs Garfield has convinced them that they are musical geniuses and, unfortunately, they take every opportunity to damage the ears of those unlucky enough to be obliged to listen to them.'

'I beg your pardon, sir, for inadvertently comparing your daughters to cats. Shall we remain here until the performance is over?'

With a heavy sigh Mr Garfield shook his head and slowly

regained his feet. 'They are not bad girls; I love them both dearly, but they are being ridiculed for their lack of talent and excess of enthusiasm. I have not the heart to tell them, but I wish someone else would, even if it causes them temporary embarrassment.'

Jonathan was not about to volunteer for this unpleasant task, but he would ask Georgiana if she could tactfully suggest the girls were not as talented as they thought. 'Are you intending to make a long stay with Sir Matthew?'

'A sennight, no longer. He is my wife's brother-in-law, no relation of mine. I like Sir Matthew and Lady Rawlings, and his daughters are well behaved young ladies.' His smile slipped a little. 'My boy, George, is much taken with Sir Matthew's eldest, Peter, but I think he is a bad influence. He has been given too much leeway, if you want to know my opinion.'

The dreadful cacophony echoed down the passageway and Jonathan winced. Only the most besotted of parents would imagine the racket to be tuneful. If Darcy did not put a stop to it, then he would do so. The Garfield girls did not deserve to be humiliated any further. He entered the music room to find the gentlemen who had preceded him were strolling towards the ladies at the far end. Nobody had intervened.

He straightened his shoulders, took a deep breath and marched smartly towards the two girls who were apparently oblivious to the mass hilarity they were engendering. He halted beside them – still they continued their performance, despite the fact that he was standing no more than an arm's length from the two of them.

There was nothing for it. He must speak to them. He cleared his throat noisily to no avail. 'Excuse me, ladies...' He could think of nothing else to say that would not be unkind. Happily, his raised voice had the desired effect, and Miss

Garfield froze in mid-note and her sister's hands dropped away from the harp strings. They looked at him expectantly but his mind had emptied of coherent thought. Jonathan ran a finger around his stock, which had become unaccountably tight.

'Miss Garfield, Miss Emily, we are about to play charades and I would so like to have you both join in.' Georgiana had come to his rescue.

'Miss Darcy, I cannot tell you how much I'm looking forward to this activity. I have not played charades since I was a boy at home, but no doubt the ability will not have deserted me.'

'Oh, thank you so much for fetching us. We should have hated to have missed the opportunity to participate.' Miss Garfield beamed. 'When we are playing together I am afraid that we become immersed in the music.'

The young ladies happily dashed off down the room, leaving him alone with Georgiana for a moment. 'That was inspired, my dear. I do hope the rest of the party are aware they are about to play charades.'

'Unfortunately not, but I am sure Kitty will understand and smooth the matter over.' She shuddered theatrically and placed a hand on his arm. She continued, as they strolled towards the others. 'Fitzwilliam has never played in his life and I'm quite sure he will not do so now. Lizzy and Jane must not and I doubt that Mr or Mrs Garfield, or the other couple, will wish to either. That leaves ourselves, Adam and Kitty, George Garfield and his sisters. That will be more than enough to make an entertaining evening.'

As it happened the other couple were only too happy to join in the riotous game of charades. Jonathan was delighted Georgiana had suggested this, as the two Garfield girls proved themselves to be as good at acting as they had been bad at music.

Even Darcy appeared relaxed and thoroughly amused by the antics of those performing.

There had been no opportunity to converse with Georgiana alone, however, and when he said his farewells to the family and their unexpected guests he was convinced that nobody had guessed their secret. That said, it was unlikely anyone would be overly surprised when the announcement was made in a week or two.

He had committed to a summer wedding and hoped that his duties would allow him to join the Darcy family at Grosvenor Square during the next few months. He had no wish for other young bucks to stake their claim for his future wife. For his part, he would be overjoyed to tie the knot immediately, but for Georgiana's sake he hoped she would reconsider and be happy to wait at least until next year.

When he and Adam were rattling back to the Old Rectory, he was tempted to ask his friend's opinion. Adam had been a comrade in arms until he resigned his commission and took holy orders, although he had been a man of the cloth for barely six months before he renounced his calling.

From the darkness at the other side of the rocking carriage his friend spoke. 'That was a thoroughly enjoyable evening, my friend, and the next time I see Kitty it will be to marry her. I rather liked the Garfield family and the Trelawneys, which is fortunate as I heard Kitty inviting them to our wedding breakfast.'

'This is turning into a grand affair, Adam, and I had thought you wished to keep things simple.'

'It is the gentleman's part to follow and the lady's to lead when it comes to matters such as this. I care not how many attend the ceremony as long as the knot is tied. Did you know that we are to chaperone Georgiana for the Season? Our wedding trip must be postponed until late summer as Kitty does not wish to be away when her nieces or nephews are born.'

Jonathan decided now was the time to reveal his own plans. 'I have spoken to Darcy and he has given his approval to my marrying his sister. She is determined that we will be married this year, but I'm hoping to persuade her to wait until I know whether I will be in the country or not.'

'We guessed as much, but I am of the same mind as you; I would not wish to marry and then be obliged to abandon my wife for God knows how long. Why is Georgiana so set on marrying this year?'

'That is the crux of the matter. Her feelings are not in doubt, but I thought she was not prepared to marry a serving soldier and I, if I am honest, do not relish being thought of as a fortune hunter. However, she told Darcy we are to be married later this year, and I must go along with her decision.'

'Do you wish us to introduce her to suitable young men in the hope that she breaks the engagement?'

'Absolutely not!' Jonathan spoke without thinking. Then he reconsidered. 'I love her; I would be devastated if she chose someone else, but I must allow her to meet younger, richer gentlemen, and pray she stays in love with me.' His voice was gruff. 'I intend to escort her myself when I can, but you will be *in loco parentis* and must do as you see fit.'

The coach swayed to a halt and no more was said on the subject. Jonathan retired in a sombre mood. He almost wished he would be recalled to his regiment thus making his wedding impossible. Any wife would make his life more complicated, and having one as young as Georgiana would be fraught with even more problems. When commanding his men he needed to be focused, not worrying about his personal life, wondering if the woman he loved to distraction was safe somewhere behind the lines.

* * *

Lizzy climbed into bed just after midnight and Fitzwilliam joined her minutes later. 'What is the news of the two patients downstairs, my love? I had not the energy to accompany you, although I know I should have done.'

'Good news on both counts, my dear. The driver of the phaeton has regained consciousness and his companion is able to move his legs. Doctor Bevan is sanguine they will both make a full recovery. Peterson said there had been word from their families that they will be collected as soon as they are well enough to be moved.'

'What about the poor men who died? Are their cadavers to be transported elsewhere or will they be buried in the local churchyard? Why has there been so much disaster visited upon us these past months? And from what Reynolds tells me, Pemberley has always been a happy and peaceful place to live until now.'

He reached across and pulled her into his arms where she settled down with a sigh of contentment against his shoulder.

'Reynolds might believe that to be the case, darling, but I can assure you I have always felt slightly uncomfortable here. That is to say, I used to feel that way, but I now feel completely content.' He ran his hand lovingly across the bulge of her stomach. 'You have been overtaxing yourself, Lizzy, and from now on I shall insist that you spend the majority of your time with your feet up and let Georgiana and Mary do the running around for you.'

'It is a relief to have Doctor Bevan confirm our suspicions – I know there are more risks involved when carrying twins, but I am as healthy as a horse and certain nothing untoward will take place, even if our babies are delivered early.'

'The Trelawneys and Garfields are leaving first thing tomorrow, which should at least give us a few hours to recoup before the wedding the following day.'

Lizzy yawned loudly. 'I fear that Georgiana and Mary do not like each other. Your sister will miss Kitty dreadfully; they have become very close these past few months. By the by, my love, although you have agreed Georgiana can marry the major at the end of the summer, I'm hoping she will reconsider. I could not bear to lose her as well as Kitty.'

He kissed the top of her head. 'I give you my word my sister will not be leaving here this year. I shall think of a variety of incontrovertible reasons why the marriage cannot take place. Brownstone told me he is in full agreement with my schemes as he believes Georgiana should have longer to consider before launching herself into the life of a soldier's wife. I should be quite happy for them to marry next year, as one wedding in the family and three babies are more than enough for this year.'

As Lizzy was drifting off to sleep she recalled something Lydia had said. Her youngest sister had inferred that Wickham was in the vicinity visiting with friends of his family. As the wretched man had grown up in and around Pemberley this was probably the case, but she hoped Fitzwilliam did not hear of it and do something rash.

8

Georgiana could not lie in bed a moment longer; she was far too excited. The wedding ceremony was to be in their own chapel at eleven o'clock, followed by the celebratory wedding breakfast to which more than one hundred guests had been invited.

She slipped out of bed, making sure she did not awaken the bride-to-be. Kitty had slept surprisingly soundly for a young lady about to become a wife. If it was her, she was certain she would have been awake, imagining the delights or disappointments to be expected in the marriage bed.

There was little point in getting dressed as she would have to change again for the wedding. She glanced at the overmantel clock, which she could just see in the residual flickering from the fire and saw that there was no need to rouse her friend for another hour at least.

After quietly pulling on her dressing robe she crept into the sitting room and ignited several candles, using a spill pushed into the embers. The chambermaid had left sufficient coal and logs to revive the fire and within five minutes the room was pleasantly warm.

It would be light soon and no doubt there was already a hive of activity downstairs in preparation for the big event. The two injured young men were still languishing in the downstairs apartment, but they were now attended to by their own physician and family. There was more than ample room to accommodate the three extra visitors.

The cadavers of the unfortunate servants who had perished in the accident had also been removed and Pemberley was a happy place once more. She blinked back tears at the thought of those poor men and what their families would be suffering. Adam's family – she had met them the previous night – were perfectly pleasant but did not have his easy manner and she had found conversation with them somewhat stilted. Perhaps they had been overwhelmed by the magnificence of Pemberley. She smiled at this ridiculous notion – his family was as rich as Croesus and no doubt lived in a more convenient, and equally luxurious, establishment of their own.

Her opinion of Lydia had not improved with further contact but she was hopeful Mary's initial antipathy was softening somewhat. Mr Bennet had a dry wit and she was looking forward to getting to know him better after the wedding. She wasn't so sure that having Mrs Bennet with them for several weeks would be so enjoyable. Thank goodness she would be leaving for Town at the beginning of April with Adam and Kitty. Happily, Easter had been early this year and Lent was over.

It was to be hoped that Lydia would depart tomorrow morning as her presence was not conducive to a happy atmosphere. Kitty had said that Wickham was a friend of young Mr Rawlings, which was somewhat worrying as his family was attending the wedding breakfast today. From what the Garfield girls had said, Peter Rawlings was a gentleman to be avoided and she had every intention of doing so in future. A rush of happiness engulfed her at the thought that she and Jonathan would be able to announce their betrothal next week. Once this was common knowledge, she would be safe from the attentions of such ne'er-do-wells as Mr Rawlings.

'Georgiana, you have deserted me. Come back at once and keep me company.'

She rushed back into the bedchamber to find her bosom bow sitting up smiling at her, apparently not at all worried by her impending nuptials. 'I am yours to command, Miss Bennet – although by rights I should call you Miss Kitty as Mary is in residence at the moment.' She curtsied and then ran to the bell pull to summon their breakfast.

'I am so excited I could burst. I had thought I would be terrified, but I cannot tell you how eager I am to become Adam's wife.'

'You look radiant, dearest, and will be the most beautiful bride of the year. The sun is shining and there are no clouds in the sky which, I am sure, is a good omen for any wedding.'

Kitty giggled and patted the bed. 'I pity the brides who marry in the rain, for their unions are no doubt doomed. We shall have breakfast in bed today as neither of us are dressed. I don't have to wash my hair again as I did it yesterday – but I am eagerly anticipating using the bathing room again.'

'I pity the poor chambermaids today, for they will be staggering up and down the stairs with jugs of hot water all morning as all three bathing rooms will be used.'

They settled companionably together in their bed for what would be the very last time. 'I'm going to miss you sorely, Kitty. I have so enjoyed sharing my apartment with you these past months and fear I shall never have the same closeness with Mary as I have had with you.'

'At least she is speaking to you now, which is a good start. I wish she had agreed to allow Fitzwilliam to sponsor her and was accompanying us to London. Although we have all been officially out this age, not one of the Bennet girls has had a Season in London.'

'I cannot understand why your sister dresses like a poor relation and wears her hair in such an unflattering style. Despite the fact that she requires spectacles to read and play the pianoforte, I am sure there is a pretty girl beneath the unattractive exterior.'

Kitty laughed. 'If there is, I have certainly never seen it. You still have four weeks to convince her to come – at least she has agreed to have some new gowns, which will be an improvement on those that she wears presently. At almost twenty years of age she considers herself an old maid with no expectation of finding herself a husband. This is ridiculous, for with the generous dowry Fitzwilliam has supplied, even dressed as a dowd, I'm sure she will attract several eligible suitors.'

The breakfast trays arrived and conversation was temporarily halted. Once they were alone again Georgiana resumed their discussion. 'I shall look out for someone suitable this morning, as there will be a dozen or more young gentlemen attending.'

By the time they had munched their way through the contents of the trays, Annie was hovering anxiously, waiting to start preparing the bride for the ceremony. Georgiana had taken her bath the previous day so there was no urgency for her. When Kitty vanished to the bathing room, she decided to check that their ensembles were perfect.

She was to wear buttercup yellow silk with a golden sarcenet overskirt. The gown had long sleeves and a high neck so there was no need for her to wear a spencer in order to keep warm in the chilly corridors. There was a swirl of silk roses around the neckline and these were echoed on the silk underskirt.

The gown Kitty had selected for her nuptials was far less ornate – it was made from a heavy, cream silk and had a demi-train. The neck was square-cut so the topaz jewellery, given to her by Adam, would be shown to advantage. It was a spectacular dress and Kitty was going to make a most beautiful bride.

Ellie, her personal maid, was eager to begin preparing her mistress for the grand event. 'Miss Darcy, it will take me ever so long to put up your hair and thread the ribbons through it. Shall I start now so you are done when Miss Bennet returns?'

'Very well, it would do no harm to get my hair arranged, but I have no wish to get dressed just yet – I cannot sit in my gown as it will crease fearfully.' Obediently she settled on the stool in front of the dressing table and resigned herself to sitting still for at least an hour.

* * *

Lizzy viewed the gown she was holding out in front of the long glass with dismay. 'Fitzwilliam, I had no idea my bump had grown so much in the past two weeks. This gown will not do; I have quite outgrown it.'

Her husband, who was lounging in an armchair in the sitting room, looked unperturbed by her disastrous discovery. 'My darling, you have a closet full of delightful ensembles – surely there is something amongst them that will do instead?'

'Fitzwilliam, I had not thought you a man of little intellect.' His feet swung to the floor. She had his full attention now. 'If this gown is too small, why should the others be any larger?'

'Devil take it! Is there nothing with a fuller skirt amongst the dozens you have?'

'It is the bodice that is too small, my love, and they are all of a similar size. I really should have thought of this before, as it is too late to have anything altered now.' She was not given to displays of hysteria, but was sorely tempted to dissolve into tears and wring her hands.

On seeing her distress he was beside her in a second, and the comfort of his arms around her restored her composure. 'Come, sweetheart, we shall look together. I care not what you wear as long as you are at my side.'

She rested her cheek on his shoulder. She loved him dearly, but he failed to see the enormity of the situation. Like most gentlemen he viewed clothes as something one wore, not as a statement of prestige. For Mrs Darcy of Pemberley to appear in anything but the finest was unthinkable.

With a sigh she pushed herself away. 'There is no need for you to trouble yourself, Fitzwilliam. My abigail is the best one to search out something suitable. Why don't you join the gentlemen in the billiard room? I shall be there as soon as I am ready.'

'If you are sure you do not need my assistance, I shall do as you suggest. It would do no harm to stroll around the place and make sure that everything is as it should be.' He seemed remarkably reluctant to leave their apartment – there was something else keeping him here.

'What is it you are not telling me, my love? You have been decidedly edgy since my family arrived.' No sooner had she spoken the words than she understood his dithering. 'My mother and Lydia will not be downstairs; they will remain in their rooms until they can make a suitable entrance. Kitty made it quite clear she did not require Mama's assistance in her own preparations, so at least I am sanguine she is safe from interference this morning.'

He looked a trifle shamefaced that his avoidance of her parent had been discovered. 'I have no objection to Mrs Bennet

– she is a good-hearted lady – but I find Mrs Wickham not to my taste. I fear I made an error of judgement allowing her to attend the wedding.'

'I believe that Kitty also wishes she had not asked you to rescind your previous decision and allow her to come here. Mama is the only one who fails to see the flaws in Lydia's character and still holds my youngest sister as her favourite.' She paused, not sure she should pass on the information she had received from Kitty.

'Is there something troubling you, Lizzy? You must tell me. I will not have you worrying in your condition.'

'Wickham is staying with the Rawlings family. I have a dreadful feeling he might have the temerity to accompany them to the wedding today.'

'That rogue will set foot on Pemberley over my dead body.' Without a further word he strode from the room and her heart sank to her toes. He was implacable in his hatred of George Wickham and she had a lowering feeling that her beloved husband might do something catastrophic and ruin Kitty's wedding.

Her worries about her appearance were nothing compared to this. Sarah, her maid, peered nervously around the door. She would never enter when Fitzwilliam was there.

'Madam, I have been going through your wardrobe and believe I have found two gowns that will still fit. Both are smart enough for today and you have gloves and slippers to match both.'

Lizzy was no longer interested in her garments, and she wished to get downstairs as soon as possible and attempt to divert disaster. If Wickham arrived she would not put it past her husband to have him thrown bodily from the premises in front of the assembled guests.

* * *

Jonathan had been ready to depart for Pemberley an hour before his friend. He had never seen Adam so jumpy; matrimony appeared to scare him more than facing a brigade of enemy soldiers. He wandered around the premises doing the pretty with Adam's ancient aunts and his sister-in-law.

Eventually the party was assembled and the three carriages ready to depart. He was to travel in the first with Adam, and the others would come in the remaining vehicles.

'Do you have the rings, Jonathan?'

'I do, and you have asked me that question three times already. You must steady your nerves, old fellow, or you will make a cake of yourself at the ceremony.'

'I know it is ridiculous, but I keep imagining myself standing alone at the altar, that Kitty has jilted me. I shall not be relaxed until I see her coming down the aisle on Mr Bennet's arm.'

'She will be there, and will be as nervous as you. You are taking a step that will change both your lives and it is only to be expected that you are somewhat unsettled at the prospect.'

'I wish we hadn't invited so many to the breakfast. Serving wine and champagne so early in the day is a recipe for disaster. Remember what happened at the party before Christmas? Those same young gentlemen, and several more, will be attending.'

'I give you my word, Adam, that I'll keep an eye on them myself. There will be no repeat of their misbehaviour.' He patted his best dress uniform and rattled his sword. 'I defy any of them to misbehave when faced with such a formidable character as myself.' His light-hearted comment failed to reassure his friend.

'There is something you do not know about the family. I'm

not sure I should tell you, as you are somewhat involved with one of the parties. However, in the circumstances I think it best you know.'

He listened with incredulity at how Wickham had behaved towards his future wife, and the disrespectful way he'd treated Lydia Bennet, and understood his friend's concern.

'I only heard this myself an hour ago, or I would have sent a note warning Sir Matthew not to include Wickham in his party today. There will be trouble if he does, and it is not the young sprigs you should be concerned about, but Darcy.'

'It is unfortunate that Kitty insisted Lydia should attend her wedding. She regrets it now, but too late for retractions. You must give me your word you will keep Darcy from doing anything he might later regret. The last thing Kitty and I require is fisticuffs at our wedding.'

'I take it Wickham is well aware he is *persona non grata* at Pemberley? Surely he would not be so imbecilic as to intrude where he is not wanted?'

'From what I've heard about him, he has no scruples and will do whatever will best serve his own interests.'

'If Darcy has his men waylay the Rawlings family coach before it arrives, an unpleasant situation could be averted.'

'You must find Darcy as soon as we arrive and make sure he is aware Wickham could be arriving unannounced and uninvited.'

The carriage lapsed into contemplative silence and Jonathan could think of nothing to add to the conversation that would make the situation more tolerable. The remaining miles gave him ample opportunity to consider what he had just learnt about his future wife. This was something he could not mention to Georgiana; he must wait for her to tell him herself.

Her near abduction had taken place when she was still in

the schoolroom, and as far as he was concerned she was the innocent party and no blame lay at her feet. However, if he got the opportunity he would enjoy punching Wickham on the nose – but not today – retribution would have to wait, as he had no intention of ruining the wedding of his closest comrade.

9

Georgiana followed Kitty down the aisle as she walked demurely on the arm of Mr Bennet. Only as she was sitting in the pew on the left with the remainder of the Bennet family, and Fitzwilliam and Bingley, did she consider how Mary was feeling after having been ignored by her sister.

By rights it should have been Mary who assisted the bride and Kitty should have suggested that she relinquish her role. Adam and Jonathan were standing side by side and although Adam was not in regimentals, it was obvious he had been a soldier most of his life.

Her heart skipped a beat when she saw Jonathan, magnificent in his dark blue uniform. The gold epaulettes, and frogging across his chest served to emphasise the width of his shoulders and made him look even more handsome – if that were possible. He was holding his peaked shako under his arm and he was also wearing his dress sword. This must be the first time such a weapon had been seen in the Pemberley Chapel, at least in living memory.

Somehow sensing her glance he looked across the church and the hard planes of his face softened. The smile he gave her would leave no one in any doubt that they were in love. The service was about to commence and his eyes were once more to the front.

As she listened to the beautiful words and heard Adam and Kitty make their responses so confidently, her heart filled with happiness. In a few short months she too would be standing beside the man she loved repeating the well-known phrases in the very same place.

Too soon it was over, the rings were exchanged, and Kitty was now Mrs Adam King and no longer her confidante. From now on Kitty's allegiance would be to Adam, as it should be. The congregation stood up and the sound of the harpsichord filled the chapel whilst the bride and groom began their stately procession down the aisle to the applause of the congregation.

Only the immediate family had been invited to the ceremony itself, but there were to be over one hundred extra guests for the wedding breakfast.

Jonathan stopped at the end of her pew and she stepped out and placed her hand on his arm. She smiled shyly up at him. 'Just think, my love, we shall be exchanging our vows here at the end of the summer, God willing.'

His eyes blazed down. 'I cannot wait, sweetheart, and I'm sorely tempted to demand that Darcy withdraws his permission for you to go to Town. The thought of you being pestered by more eligible, younger gentlemen fills me with horror.'

'It matters not who I am introduced to; I have given you my heart and am not interested in anyone else. You may rest easy, Jonathan. I am going merely to enjoy the spectacle. Fitzwilliam has agreed to announce our betrothal before I leave, so I shall not have to attend Almack's and parade around the place like a brood mare at a horse sale, for which I am thankful.'

Kitty and Adam were now just ahead of them and about to turn onto the central flagstone corridor that bisected Pemberley, when they halted. Kitty put her arms around Adam's neck and he crushed her to his chest as they embraced.

Such a display in public was unheard of, but Georgiana envied her friend. Jonathan's hand closed over hers. 'That will be us, my darling, very soon. I cannot wait to make you my wife.' This was said quietly, for her ears alone. Then, he raised his voice. 'Enough of that, Mr King – you are giving Miss Darcy palpitations.'

Adam released his bride and both he and Kitty turned to face them. 'Miss Darcy, I humbly apologise for being so bold as to kiss Mrs King.'

Kitty ran to her side. 'This is the happiest day of my life, dearest friend, and I care not what the old tabbies say. I am now a respectable married woman and shall do as I please.'

'Will you now? I believe I might have something to say on the matter if you do.' Adam took Kitty's hand again and the four of them continued towards the Grand Staircase where the expected guests would be greeted.

Fitzwilliam and Lizzy arrived. 'We are tardy; people are already arriving. Georgiana, will you and the major remain in the Great Hall and ensure that everything is running smoothly? Lizzy and I will be fully occupied with King and Kitty for the next hour.' Her brother appeared remarkably relaxed for a gentleman who was not overfond of large social gatherings.

'Of course we will, Fitzwilliam. I shall introduce the new arrivals to Mr and Mrs Bennet and the King family.'

There was a sumptuous buffet set out in the music room and

this would be available as soon as the bride and groom returned. Today they were not only serving champagne and hot punch, but also tea and coffee. This was a departure from tradition but Lizzy had thought non-alcoholic alternatives should be available so early in the day.

She and Jonathan were the first to arrive and they were greeted by the sounds of a small orchestra playing on a rostrum that had been set up at the far end of the Great Hall. 'Everything is quite perfect, apart from the fact that this room is unpleasantly cold. I am so glad we have decided to marry when the weather is more clement.'

He guided her to the centre of the vast space before answering. 'Once everyone is here it will be warm enough.' He patted his splendid jacket. 'My uniform is far thicker than your gown and when you are comfortable I shall be sweltering.'

'I am astonished that you do not trip yourself up with that sword at your waist. I sincerely hope it remains firmly in its scabbard.' No sooner had she spoken than she regretted her playful remark as his eyes narrowed and for a second he was unrecognisable. 'What is it? Why do you look like that?'

He was staring at the entrance through which guests would be arriving at any moment. His forearm was rigid beneath her gloved fingers – there was something amiss and she wished to know what it was.

'Jonathan, tell me at once – what is wrong?'

'I have no wish to alarm you, sweetheart, but I fear that Wickham might try and intrude on this celebration.'

Her joy in the day ended. 'Fitzwilliam will do something regrettable if he does. The fact that you are so angry must mean that you know what happened in Brighton.'

Instantly his expression changed and he smiled down at her with such love that for a second she forgot the dreadful news. 'I do, my darling, but I care not for your part in it. However, that rogue will regret it if I ever come face to face with him.'

'I don't understand why Wickham should wish to intrude. I knew he was in the neighbourhood – after all he grew up here – so why would he be so foolhardy as to provoke my brother in this way?'

'I sincerely hope you are right, but he is staying with the young Rawlings and they can hardly leave him on his own. Do you think they are aware that he is not welcome at Pemberley?'

'I don't know – I doubt it. Although they were invited to the Christmas party they are merely acquaintances, not close friends of ours. I think that my brother is making an effort to be more sociable for Lizzy's sake, but I cannot remember any occasion where the Rawlings family and the Darcys were together in either house. I have been to their annual garden party on two occasions, but never to a formal event.'

His grim expression returned. 'In which case, my love, I had better abandon you and station myself outside in case he turns up with them. They can hardly leave him kicking his heels if he is their guest, and he probably thinks Darcy will not make a fuss in front of his neighbours.'

'Please go. Jane and Bingley are here now and they can help with the introductions as they met many of the people last year.' She watched him stride away; he was obviously unaware what a striking figure he made, or that both gentlemen and ladies stepped aside to clear his path without him needing to ask.

* * *

Lizzy gently touched her husband's arm. 'Fitzwilliam, you must smile. Your forbidding expression is not acceptable at such a happy occasion.' She had expected him to smile and relax his rigid stance, but instead he looked even more fierce. 'What is it? Surely you do not think Wickham would be so foolish as to come here today?'

'I cannot get the thought from my head; I should be outside making sure. I have two of my men on alert, but I could hardly inform the rest of my staff as they have no notion why he is forbidden to visit.'

'Look, Major Brownstone is approaching and he appears equally grim.'

'Darcy, I'm going to wait outside. I give you my word he will not get past me.'

'Major, remember that if you do anything extraordinary it will be the talk of the county by this evening.'

'I understand that perfectly, Mrs Darcy. I have no intention of running him through, however tempted I might be. There will be the minimum of fuss and no scandal at all.'

'In which case, sir, I thank you for your help. Now, Fitzwilliam, you can relax and greet the guests without putting them off their breakfast with your scowl.'

Finally he smiled, just in time, as the first arrivals were being ushered through the doors at that very moment. The major strode off and she tried to push away the sense of foreboding she had woken with this morning. Georgiana's future husband was a capable man, a military man, and would make sure nothing untoward took place to spoil her sister's wedding day.

* * *

Jonathan had never met Wickham, but he knew the Rawlings family by sight and had a pretty good description of the man he sought. Hopefully this would be sufficient to avoid him accosting a total stranger.

He could hardly stand around in the turning circle. He was too conspicuous in his uniform, so he had better stride about the place as if he needed fresh air or to blow a cloud. Perhaps he could lurk on the terrace and still be able to see the occupants of the coaches and carriages as they trundled down the drive.

From his vantage point, at the extreme corner of the flagstone terrace, he was able to see well enough without being observed himself. The first carriage contained the Garfields. He recognised Miss Emily who was sitting on the side of the vehicle nearest to him.

The next two were occupied by families he did not know, but the following coaches contained the family he sought. Time to make himself visible. He wouldn't know if Wickham was within one of the vehicles until the occupants descended.

His instinct was to move directly to the turning circle, but he thought it might be better to stroll across as if he was there by happenstance. He nodded and smiled at the ladies and gentlemen, all dressed in their finest, who were moving towards the open double doors and into the house. He stiffened as a man in riding clothes appeared at his shoulder.

'Major Brownstone, I am Ingram, steward at Pemberley. If the bastard is within either coach, we should be able to bundle him away before he sets foot inside.'

'Good man. I'm relieved you are here as I have been having doubts about my ability to distinguish him from the others. There seem to be an inordinate number of gentlemen in the second vehicle – I fear that Sir Matthew has brought more than one uninvited guest with him.' This second carriage had to wait until the first had moved away which meant, with luck, that the ladies of the party would already be inside before there was any unpleasantness.

He nodded and smiled at Lady Rawlings as she and her

daughters fluttered past. Sir Matthew hesitated when he saw them both and then stepped over in their direction.

'This looks like a reception party, gentlemen. Did you wish to speak to me or is it my son and his friends you are waiting for?'

For a moment they were hidden from the second coach by the first one moving off. 'Sir Matthew, is Wickham with your party?' The man nodded. 'I fear he is not welcome here and we have been sent to make sure he does not set foot in the house. He and Darcy have unsettled business between them. If they were to meet, there will be violence.'

Sir Matthew nodded. 'I don't take to the fellow, but my son would include him and his other cronies. I shall wait with you. There is less likely to be trouble if I am here as well.'

Two well-drilled footmen stepped forward to open the carriage door and let down the steps. First to emerge was Peter Rawlings, and his habitual sneer slipped when he saw there was a reception committee.

Before he could warn the others his father grabbed his son's elbow and hissed something into his ear that Jonathan could not follow. Immediately Rawlings dashed away, not giving a second thought to those he had invited to accompany him.

'It will be better to refuse entry to all three of them, not draw attention to Wickham,' Jonathan said.

'Good idea, Major Brownstone,' Sir Matthew replied. 'I should not have let my wife persuade me to include them, as I knew they had not been invited.'

Jonathan moved swiftly to the carriage door and kicked the steps back before the occupants could emerge. His bulk filled the door and prevented them from escaping. Ingram was now standing with his back to the other door, making sure they did not exit that way.

'Gentlemen, I fear there has been a misunderstanding. This is a private affair and by invitation only. The carriage will return you to Carstairs House immediately. I apologise for the inconvenience, but I'm sure that you understand why you cannot attend this wedding breakfast.'

Two of the young men shrugged and settled back without a murmur but the third, a handsome, hard-faced, older individual was not so easily placated. 'I am a member of this family. My wife is sister to Mrs Darcy and this embargo does not apply to me.'

Without a second thought Jonathan reached in and grasped Wickham by his cravat and twisted it hard. 'You are not welcome here, and neither is your wife. She will be departing Pemberley immediately. Come here again and I will not be answerable for my actions.'

He twisted the cloth again and his captive turned a satisfying shade of beetroot. Then as he released his hold, Jonathan shoved him, and Wickham sprawled in a heap on the floor of the carriage.

The bastard's face contorted with rage. 'No one treats me like this and gets away with it. You will live to regret your actions today, be very sure of this.'

Jonathan slammed the door and gestured to the driver to move away. He should not have laid hands on Wickham. The plan had been to prevent him from entering – no more than that. He shrugged. The man was of no consequence; his duty was done and he could return to the celebration confident there would be no unpleasantness to spoil the day.

Sir Matthew followed him in. 'Do not fear, sir, I shall send Wickham packing on my return. He will not be welcome at Carstairs House again.'

'Mrs Wickham is to leave here directly after the breakfast.

She is to borrow the Bennet coach for her journey. How did her husband arrive at your establishment?'

'My son collected him from the coaching inn at Bakewell. He has been with us for two days and my daughters and Lady Rawlings are besotted with him, but he set my teeth on edge. I don't take to a man who smiles too much.'

'Might I suggest, Sir Matthew, that this remains between us? Hopefully your son will have the sense to keep quiet as well – after all, he should have known better than to invite his friends to a private event.'

'I shall have a word with him immediately. He has been indulged by his mother and I have turned a blind eye to his foibles. This stops today. Excuse me, Major, I must find him before he causes more problems.'

The confrontation with Wickham had taken little time. The coaches waiting behind to disgorge their passengers would scarcely have been aware that anything untoward had taken place. He looked towards Darcy and nodded, pleased to see his future brother-in-law respond with a smile.

The guests did not dally in the spacious, but cold, entrance hall, but were immediately guided to an anteroom where they could remove their outer garments before joining the throng in the Great Hall. He headed for this chamber, eagerly anticipating spending time with Georgiana who looked *ravissante* in her finery.

He paused in the double doorway to scan the crowds and was immediately aware there was something not quite right. He was used to being stared at; he was a tall man with a shock of conker-coloured hair, and when wearing his uniform he could not fail to be the centre of attention.

However, the surreptitious glances he was getting were different from the usual. Then Georgiana saw him and with a slight flick of her hand indicated he should retire and that she would join him. He had a horrible suspicion that Rawlings had been spreading gossip – and blackening his name.

He retreated and made his way to the large anteroom in which he and Georgiana had met before.

10

Georgiana saw Lydia approaching her with Rawlings in tow. These were the last two people she wished to converse with on such a happy occasion.

'Mrs Wickham, Mr Rawlings, how can I be of assistance?'

'Mr Rawlings has had the most unpleasant experience and it is your fault, Miss Darcy. Major Brownstone has caused him a great deal of embarrassment by his behaviour.'

'I cannot imagine why you think that anything the major has done is in any way my concern.' Georgiana stared frostily at Rawlings. 'Neither is it any of my concern whether Mr Rawlings has been embarrassed or not.'

The gentleman in question glared at her with such venom that for a moment she was quite disconcerted, then she rallied – after all he was no threat to her, for she had Jonathan to protect her.

Lydia was not to be deterred. 'My dear Wickham and two of Mr Rawlings' closest friends intended to call in to pay their respects to the bride and groom – no more than that – I can assure you. However, your Major Brownstone took it into his head to assault my husband and refused to let any of them come in.'

This was news indeed. She drew herself straight and fixed them with a steely gaze. 'Mrs Wickham, you are as well aware as I am that your husband is not welcome here – indeed, madam, neither are you. This is a private party and you, Mr Rawlings, have no right to include your friends in your own invitation.'

Although she had kept her voice low, her rigid stance was beginning to draw unwelcome attention from other guests. 'I suggest, Mrs Wickham, that you retire to your room and begin packing, for you will be leaving Pemberley as soon as I have spoken to my brother.'

She turned her back on them and was at a loss as to what to do next. She could hardly interrupt Fitzwilliam whilst he was welcoming the remainder of the guests. Her heart was thumping uncomfortably and her hands were clammy – she did so dislike falling out with somebody, however well-deserved.

To her delight she saw Jonathan appear in the doorway; he would know what to do to defuse the matter, for she was certain both Lydia and Rawlings had already been telling their tale of woe to anyone who was prepared to listen.

She gestured to him, and he understood immediately and disappeared from view. She hurried after him, certain he would go to the chamber they had used last time to converse. It was as if two dozen pairs of eyes were burning into her back and this was an uncomfortable feeling.

As she'd hoped, he was waiting and she wanted to throw herself into his arms but managed to restrain this immodest impulse. Until they were officially betrothed she must do nothing to draw attention to herself.

He stepped aside and she dashed past, noticing that he left the door wide open so that could there be no hint of impropriety in their clandestine meeting. 'Jonathan, Lydia and Rawlings are causing trouble and I fear that I have made things so much worse.'

'You must tell me exactly what happened, sweetheart, but first I will explain what I did.'

When he had completed his story she nodded. 'It is as I thought, my love, and you have done nothing anyone could take exception to. Wickham knows that he is not permitted to set foot here, so he has only himself to blame if he was manhandled. If my brother had seen him, he would have fared much worse.'

'I'm sure that is the case. However, we have poked a hornets' nest and must do our best to calm the situation before Kitty and Adam hear of it.' His expression was serious as he continued. 'I fear that Mrs Bennet will take her daughter's side, and Lady Rawlings will do the same with her son. Mr Bennet and Sir Matthew will not cavil, but unfortunately, it is not the gentlemen who gossip and cause trouble.'

The sound of voices and laughter outside indicated the last of the guests were making their way to the Great Hall. 'We must waylay Fitzwilliam and tell him what has happened.'

'There is no need, my dear, Sir Matthew has already apprised us of what took place.' Her brother, accompanied by Lizzy and the bride and groom, stepped into the anteroom.

Georgiana rushed to Kitty and took her hands. 'I cannot tell you how sorry I am that...'

'You have nothing to be sorry about; this whole debacle is entirely my fault. I should never have pressed for Lydia to be included in the invitation.' Her friend looked remarkably unbothered by this distressing situation.

'If blame is to be laid anywhere it is with Wickham himself,' Adam said firmly. 'And young Rawlings is not a nincompoop; he must have known his friends were not invited and so should not have brought them with him.'

'I told Lydia that she must leave immediately – I hope I have not taken too much upon myself.'

Her brother opened his arms and she flung herself into them. He held her close for a moment and rubbed her back as if she were a small child, before releasing her. 'Lizzy has already put matters in motion, and the Bennet carriage is being put to as we speak. Now, we must join the party and ignore any innuendos. I shall speak to the senior gentlemen and Lizzy will do the same with the matrons. It is immaterial what the young ladies and gentlemen say.'

Georgiana was reassured. 'From what I have heard, Mr Rawlings is not popular, especially with the ladies. That's hardly surprising if he has such unpleasant friends. I expect the other two were the same gentlemen who caused the unpleasantness at the party before Christmas.'

Fitzwilliam looked at Lizzy and she nodded. 'Georgiana, I have decided to announce your betrothal immediately. We think it best that all concerned are aware that Major Brownstone was acting on my behalf as a member of the Darcy family.'

'Kitty, are you quite sure you do not mind? I have no wish to intrude on your special day.'

'Don't be a goose, knowing my dearest friend is to be married will make my day even more perfect. Come along, everyone, I cannot wait to share this exciting news. Once the announcement is made the petty gossip will be forgotten.'

* * *

Lizzy touched Kitty's arm, indicating she wished to speak to her privately, and immediately her sister released Adam's hand and fell in beside her. 'What is it, Lizzy? Are you unwell?'

'No, but I fear there will be ructions from Mama. Do you think you could find Jane and Mary and get their assistance to divert a scene? Lydia has always been Mama's favourite and I am sure she will not take kindly to this supposed slight, nor will she be happy that Wickham was so rudely treated.'

'I shall find them at once. No one will think it strange of me as the bride is supposed to circulate amongst her guests, is she not? You have more than enough to do if you are to speak to Mrs Garfield and the other ladies.'

Although Lizzy had said she was not feeling unwell, this was not entirely true as the babies were more vigorous than usual and the sensation was becoming uncomfortable. She viewed the throng of guests with dismay. Trying to find anyone in such a crush was going to be difficult.

Then Fitzwilliam was beside her, his arm around her waist and his face deeply etched with concern. 'This is too much for you. I should not have asked you to become involved in your condition. Come with me; I shall escort you to our apartment where you must rest with your feet up until you feel better.'

'How did you know I was feeling fatigued? I told Kitty I was perfectly fine.'

His smile, despite her ever-increasing size, still made her heart beat faster. 'I have you in my view at all times, my love, and could tell at once that you were in need of my assistance.' He guided her through the crowd and across the flagstone passageway to the secondary stairs. The carved oak staircase was equally impressive as the marble stairs, but they were not used as much as they led directly to the guest wing and not to the main part of the house.

As soon as they were away from the noise, Fitzwilliam bent

and slipped his arm around her knees and scooped her up. 'I am far too heavy for you to carry all that way. I shudder to think how much weight I have put on these past few months.'

'A mere bagatelle, my darling. Hold tight and I shall have you in our apartment in a trice.' He suited his actions to his words and bounded up the stairs, along several corridors until he burst into their shared apartment.

'I have no wish to go to bed, Fitzwilliam. I shall rest on the *chaise longue* for a while and then rejoin you.'

He placed her tenderly on the daybed and fussed with her pillows as if he were her maid. When he was satisfied she was comfortable he stepped back. 'I insist that you remain where you are until I come and see you again in a little while. You must take no risks with your health or that of our babies – Kitty and King understand the situation and will not be offended at your absence.'

'Perhaps Jane will come up and join me here. Although she is not like a beached whale, she is noticeably with child and I'm sure Bingley would be pleased if she rested as well.'

'Excellent notion, my love. I shall also have trays sent up for you so you will not miss any of the splendid buffet. Cook has surpassed herself again and even with your meagre appetite, I'm sure there will be something you will enjoy.'

He leaned down and kissed her, his lips firm on hers, and not for the first time she wished she was less ungainly and they could resume the intimacies of the marriage bed.

After he left, she closed her eyes and dozed but was jerked awake when her sitting room door crashed open. She sat up, her heart racing to find Lydia and her mother already inside her private sanctum without being given leave to enter.

Without preamble her sibling launched into a tirade. 'I hope you're satisfied, Lizzy. Your husband is turning me out as if I was of no account and not his sister. You have ruined this day for me and your family. We are leaving immediately and Mary and Papa are coming too.'

Before Lizzy could frame a suitably crushing reply, her mother chimed in. 'A viper in my bosom! You are an unnatural daughter and I shall no longer call you a member of this family. To think I was pleased to have Mr Darcy as my son – he has not changed one iota. He is proud and disdainful and you are prejudiced against Lydia and her dearest Wickham.'

Mama had not bothered to lower her voice and her strident tones brought both her own maid and her chambermaid running into the room. This would not do. Lizzy was the chatelaine of Pemberley and would not be spoken to in this way by anyone – even her own mother.

'I have heard quite enough, thank you, from both of you. Lydia, you are well aware why neither you nor Wickham are welcome here or at Longbourn. Mr Darcy only allowed you to come here because Kitty wanted all her family to see her marry.' Slowly she pushed herself to her feet and faced her accusers. 'Your bags are already being packed, Lydia, and if you wish to leave as well, Mama, then so be it. However, Mary and Papa are remaining with us.'

'They will not wish to do so once they hear how poorly you have treated me,' Lydia shrieked.

Her mother was incoherent with anger but finally managed to vent her spleen. 'You are coming between a man and his wife, Mrs Darcy, and that is against the church and common decency. Lydia and I shall go. Be very sure we will never return here even if you beg us to. Do not be surprised if Mr Collins hears about this and decides to evict us. You will have made us homeless as well as separating Mr Bennet from myself.'

This whole debacle was becoming tiresome but Lizzy could

see no way of ending it unless she was as uncivil as her sister and her mother. Then Fitzwilliam appeared, his face a mask of fury.

'Remove yourself from my private apartment, madam. Your carriage is waiting and your trunks are already inside. You will leave my house this instant. Do I make myself clear?'

Both Lydia and her mother visibly shrunk at his tone. Without a further remark they turned and fled and Lizzy's legs gave way beneath her. This time her husband was not fast enough to catch her and she collapsed in an ungainly heap on the carpet.

'God dammit to hell! Here, darling, let me help you up. If I had known those two termagants would accost you here I would never have left you alone.' He put his arm around her waist and gently raised her to her feet.

'I have no wish to retire, my love. I shall remain on the daybed. If it was not so distressing, I would find the situation amusing. It is like something out of a Gothic romance – you casting the villains out into the cold in so dramatic a fashion.'

Once she was comfortably settled, and her feet resting on a cushion, he pulled up a chair and sat beside her. 'I spoke to Mary and Mr Bennet and they wish to remain here and not be associated with this incident. You will be relieved to know that things are comfortable again downstairs. Sir Matthew has sent his wife and his son away and this was sufficient to quash the rumours and gossip. I intend to announce Georgiana's engagement after everyone has eaten their fill.'

'I should like to come down for that; in fact, now I know Lydia and the unpleasant Rawlings boy have gone I feel much better. I am sorry that my mother behaved so appallingly. She will not be welcome here again.'

He took her hands and raised them to his lips and gently

kissed her knuckles. 'She is your mother, sweetheart. You must not cut her off entirely. She will be our babies' grandmother. Although not ideal, she is the only one they will have.'

Lizzy looked at him with surprise. 'Are you saying you would be prepared to have her back after what she has said and done this morning?'

He nodded. 'Of course I would, but I will be guided by you. Until you are ready to see her again she will remain at Longbourn. However, Mrs Wickham is another matter – she shall not visit Pemberley under any circumstances.'

As he spoke she knew in her heart that she would never see her youngest sister again, and although sad at the prospect, she could not help but feel relieved. Lydia had always been out of step with her sisters, behaving like a member of the demimonde, and after she married Wickham she had no chance of improving her character.

* * *

Georgiana noticed Sir Matthew speaking to his wife and son very sternly and then the two of them slunk off – no sooner had this happened than the atmosphere in the room improved. 'Have you seen Mrs Bennet or Lydia, Jonathan? I shall not be sanguine until I'm sure they are not down here causing trouble for Kitty and Adam.'

From his high vantage point he gazed over the heads of the guests and shook his head. 'No, they appear to have gone. Just a moment, I see that your butler is talking most urgently to Darcy.'

'I hope Lizzy is not unwell; Peterson looks most concerned. Do you think we should follow and see if we can be of assistance?'

'No, Darcy doesn't look worried but furious. Best to leave him to it. Shall we circulate, my love? I have yet to meet all your friends and acquaintances.'

They spent a pleasant half an hour together and then the doors to the music room were flung open and the guests surged forward. The food at Pemberley was legendary and all wished to be the first to try the lobster patties, white soup, fricassee of chicken and other delicacies.

'I think I would prefer to wait for a while before eating, Jonathan. There are far too many people queueing at the buffet table.' Sufficient tables and chairs had been laid out, with the best crystalware and silver cutlery, to accommodate everybody. No one would be obliged to stand about with a plate in one hand and a glass in the other today.

'Shall we take a stroll until we can go in, Georgiana? I am becoming somewhat overheated and it is cold enough out there to restore my composure.'

She giggled at the thought that a soldier could become overheated and uncomfortable, for this was normally the prerogative of the young ladies. 'I should enjoy that, my love, and I have no wish for you to suffer from a fit of the vapours.'

'Saucy minx! We have much to discuss before the announcement is made later. For one, do you wish to replicate today for our own nuptials or did you have something else in mind?'

'I thought a garden party would be perfect. We can still be married in this chapel, but we can have our wedding breakfast in the garden.'

They had reached the marble staircase when two cloaked figures began their descent. Georgiana saw that it was Mrs Bennet and Lydia Wickham. She tried to retreat before they saw her, but she was too late.

11

Luckily, the vast entrance hall was empty of guests apart from themselves, Mrs Wickham and Mrs Bennet. Of course, there were the usual sprinkling of footmen standing to attention by the walls and doors, but these did not count as they were loyal and would not gossip. Jonathan had his arm around Georgiana's waist and moved her smartly in behind him. Attack was always better than retreat, in his opinion.

'Mrs Bennet, Mrs Wickham, your carriage is waiting outside. I suggest that you do not keep the horses standing.'

The redoubtable matron flushed and lowered her eyes – one foe vanquished – but he thought the younger woman would be harder to defeat. He fixed her with his fiercest parade-ground stare, daring her to speak. She sailed past them without uttering a word and he thought his beloved was safe from verbal abuse. Then Mrs Wickham paused at the front door and turned.

The girl's eyes were as hard as granite and she looked ten years older than her actual age. He was too far away to prevent whatever filth she intended to spew. He braced himself and wished Georgiana was elsewhere.

'I give you fair warning, Miss Darcy, that you will live to regret your actions today. Wickham and I will have our revenge – be very sure of that.'

Chasing after the wretched woman would only exacerbate the situation, the damage was done, Georgiana was ashen-faced and close to tears. Thank God the only people present had been staff, and they were loyal to the backbone to the Darcy family and not a word of what had passed would be discussed anywhere – even between themselves.

'Sweetheart, you must take no notice of that shrew. She has no other weapons to use against you but empty threats. She has been publicly humiliated and cast from the house. Small wonder she is bitter and wishes to hurt you as she has been hurt herself.'

'I pray that you are correct, but did you see her face? I have never seen such hatred and shall not be easy until I'm certain she and Wickham have left the neighbourhood.' She sniffed inelegantly and he delved into his inside pocket and handed her his handkerchief.

'They will return to Longbourn; after all, they have Mrs Bennet with them and she has no acquaintances in the area as they do. By tomorrow they will be away from here and you can be happy again. Now, I believe the crush at the buffet table has eased somewhat and we can find ourselves something to eat.'

Once they had filled their plates from the delicious offerings, he led her to the table at which Jane and Bingley were seated. He was pleased to see that Georgiana was now restored to high spirits and had apparently already forgotten the spiteful remarks of Mrs Wickham.

He had said that there was no substance to the threats, but the Wickhams made powerful enemies. In his opinion they were amoral and would not hesitate to hurt his lovely girl if they got the opportunity.

Bingley touched his elbow. 'My word, Brownstone, your face would curdle milk. What ails you, my friend?'

Jonathan shook off his disquiet and smiled broadly. 'Nothing at all to worry about, no doubt you will hear all about the fracas when we are just family again.'

Eventually even the greediest of guests was replete and the doors of the music room were closed, allowing the servants to clear away the debris. Everyone was ushered into the Great Hall, and Darcy and his wife joined them. Glasses were charged with the best champagne and several toasts were drunk to the bride, the groom and several other people.

Darcy looked in his direction and the time had come for him to lead Georgiana to the rostrum. Her smile was radiant. She had never looked more beautiful or more happy. He was the luckiest man in Christendom to have won her heart – not only that, but to have gained the approval of such a man as Darcy.

'Today is a very happy day, for not only have we seen Miss Catherine Bennet marry Mr King, but also I am delighted to announce the engagement between my sister, Miss Georgiana Darcy, and Major Brownstone. I ask you to raise your glasses and toast the happy couples.'

A spontaneous round of applause rippled around the room and then glasses clinked as Jonathan heard, for the first time in public, his name linked with Georgiana's.

Some time passed before he had an opportunity to take Darcy to one side and tell him what Mrs Wickham had said as she left.

'I shall send two men to follow the carriage and make sure they leave Derbyshire and do indeed return to Longbourn. Neither of the Wickhams are welcome there, but as Mr Bennet is to remain here for the next few weeks, I am sure they will ignore this embargo.'

'That is all very well, Darcy, but what about when Georgiana is in London? She will be attending routs, soirées and balls and neither you nor I shall be there to protect her. I have every faith in Adam's ability to take care of his own wife, but he is just married and his attention will be on Kitty and not Georgiana.'

'I think you are dwelling too much on the words of a spoilt young lady. Neither Lydia Wickham nor her repellent husband will be in London for the Season as they do not have the funds. Remember, Brownstone, my sister will only be moving in the highest echelons and those two would not get within one hundred yards of her. They do not move in the same circles as we do – even if they were to travel to London in the hope of spoiling Georgiana's Season, I am confident she would be safe from their machinations.'

Darcy patted him on the shoulder and moved away to mingle with the guests. Georgiana glided over and threaded her arm through his. 'You look so worried, my love. Are you already regretting your promise to marry me at the end of the summer?'

He shook off his unease. How could he be sad at such a time? 'I am still stunned that I have managed to capture the most eligible young lady in England. I do not deserve such happiness, but, sweetheart, I do not intend to cavil at my good luck.' In perfect accord they spent the remainder of the day being congratulated and exchanging pleasantries.

Adam and Kitty set off at three o'clock for the Old Rectory, leaving Adam's family and himself to stay at Pemberley. The newlyweds were to have the place to themselves; this seemed appropriate as they were not to take a honeymoon until after the delivery of the Bingley and Darcy babies.

It wasn't until he made his way to his chamber that night

that he recalled his promise to Darcy. The engagement might well be temporary as Georgiana was to be given the opportunity to meet more suitable candidates for her hand before making a final decision.

As far as she was concerned, the matter was settled and their wedding would take place in September. If she were to discover this deception, she would be appalled and no doubt demand to return home immediately and bring the wedding forward. He had given his word to stay away, to allow her to attend as many parties as she wished.

He ground his teeth at the thought of his betrothed in the arms of another man. Dammit! He cared not what he had promised Darcy, if he got furlough he would speed up to London and escort Georgiana to several events, making sure his disapproval of any importunate fortune hunters was made clear. He had yet to give her a betrothal ring – he must find out what she wanted and purchase one as soon as may be.

* * *

Georgiana believed that her apartment was less welcoming than it had been when Kitty had shared it with her. Although these chambers had been hers alone since she was old enough to come down from the nursery, they had really come alive when her dearest friend had been living with her and sharing the vast bed.

After Lydia and Mrs Bennet had departed so dramatically she had feared the wedding breakfast would be quite ruined; however, the event had been a great success. A flicker of unease ran down her spine when she recalled Lydia Wickham's final words to her.

Both Fitzwilliam and Jonathan had reassured her more than

once that she had nothing to fear, that these were mere rhetoric, that neither Mr Wickham nor his wife had the power, nor the ability to cause her any discomfort. She wriggled a little to get comfortable and pulled the warm comforter up to her chin. In six months from now it would be she who would be spending her first night as a bride and a wave of unexpected heat engulfed her at the thought of what Kitty and Adam might be doing at this very moment.

Was her future husband tossing and turning as she was? Her lips curved in the darkness. He was a soldier, no doubt he slept soundly whenever he had the opportunity. Jonathan, and Adam's family, would be leaving on the morrow, but Mary and Mr Bennet were to remain indefinitely.

Even though Mrs Bennet had accused Lizzy of coming between a husband and wife, Georgiana rather thought Mr Bennet was delighted to be given the excuse to remain at Pemberley. As she was drifting into slumber she wondered why Mary had decided stay and not leave with her mother and sister – did this mean that Kitty's sister was softening in her attitude and might eventually become a friend after all?

* * *

After a whirl of farewells the final guests had departed, leaving Georgiana and the others feeling decidedly flat. No one mentioned the absence of Mrs Bennet. It was as if she had vanished in a puff of smoke. Lizzy didn't make an appearance downstairs. On the advice of Dr Bevan she remained resting in her chamber. Carrying one baby appeared to be difficult enough, heaven knows how exhausting it must be to be having twins.

The work on the east wing had been temporarily halted

whilst there had been guests, but now the labourers, carpenters and other artisans had returned in their droves to complete the modernisation and conversion so that Jane and Bingley could make it a permanent home. Bingley, of course, was footing the bills and he and Jane were frequently to be seen in conversation with the builders and architects involved.

She wandered disconsolately around the place, wishing she had Kitty to talk to. Perhaps she would find herself an edifying book from the library and curl up on the window seat and read for an hour or two. There were to be no morning calls today; Fitzwilliam had said visitors were banned until Lizzy was feeling more the thing.

As she glided through the Great Hall the sound of music drifted towards her. She increased her pace and dashed into the music room to see that Mary was seated at the piano playing a delightful piece by Mozart that she recognised. Although the performance was not as lively as either hers or Kitty's, Mary had excellent technique and was an accomplished player.

When the last note faded, Georgiana hurried across to congratulate her. 'That was beautiful, Mary. I have never heard it played so well. Kitty told me you were a proficient performer, but it was so much more than that.'

Instead of looking pleased at the praise, Mary's lips pursed and she lowered the lid to the piano with a snap. 'You are most kind to say so, Miss Darcy. I have finished now so you are free to play yourself.' Mary had returned to her drab appearance, the finery she had worn for the wedding put aside. 'I'm going to find Mr Bennet and see if I can be of any assistance to him. He is in the library working on a scientific problem.'

'I fear that he is not where you think he is, Miss Bennet, for I saw him go out with my brother not half an hour ago. Would you care to take a turn about the grounds with me? The sun is shining and it is quite dry underfoot today.'

Mary clasped her hands under her bosom and shook her head. 'I would not dream of intruding on your promenade, Miss Darcy. I am going to retire to my room and continue with my study of the classics.' She dipped in an exaggerated curtsy and walked off with her nose in the air.

Georgiana was tempted to stick her tongue out, but decided that would be the act of a child and not a woman grown. What was wrong with the girl? Why did Mary not wish to dress in the pretty gowns that Fitzwilliam had provided for her or dress her hair in a more becoming style? She was not bracket-faced, in fact was quite pretty, but seemed determined to make the worst of herself.

The girl was halfway down the room when something prompted Georgiana to call her back. She was obliged to raise her voice in order to be heard, something Kitty was often being reprimanded for. 'Miss Bennet, Mary, do not rush away. I wish to talk to you – please join me in the small drawing room.' Her voice echoed in the vast space and the girl tripped over her feet in shock at being shouted at.

With her skirts in her hand, Georgiana ran lightly down the room and arrived in a rush at Mary's side. At least the girl had not run away, even if she had not turned or seemed particularly eager to spend time with her.

'I beg your pardon for shouting, but if I had not done so you would not have heard me. I want to be your friend, Mary. You are my sister and have come to make your home here.' Without allowing the girl to pull away, she pushed her arm through hers and all but bundled her through the huge reception rooms, down the flagstone passageway and into the more intimate, and far warmer, small drawing room.

They were quite breathless after the mad dash, but considerably warmer. 'Please forgive me, Mary, but I was determined to have you to myself today. We have much to talk about and have not had the opportunity since you arrived the other day.' Georgiana pointed to a comfortable, well-upholstered armchair to the left of the substantial fire and, before she sat down opposite, she tugged at the bell strap.

'You are quite extraordinary, Miss Darcy. I had decided to dislike you but am finding that more difficult than I thought.' Mary's face was becomingly flushed and for the first time there was the hint of a smile hovering on her lips.

'I refuse to answer to anything but my given name. You are my sister Mary and I am your sister Georgiana. Now, I intend to send for refreshments. What would you like? I intend to have coffee and whatever has been freshly baked this morning.'

'I shall have the same, thank you. I have developed a fondness for coffee but rarely have the opportunity to have it.'

A footman arrived to take their order and whilst he was there he tossed a few more logs and lumps of coal on the fire. As soon as he had left, Georgiana smiled at her companion.

'As you have now decided to almost be my friend, I'm going to speak frankly. You are a lovely young lady, why do you not let us see your beauty?'

Mary's eyes widened and her hands clenched on the arms of the chair. Was she going to rush off in high dudgeon? Then she recovered her composure and looked away as if embarrassed by what she was going to say. 'I am the plain Jane of the family. All my sisters are beautiful. I am obliged to wear spectacles in order to see and possess neither wit nor charm to compensate for my lack of countenance. I have endeavoured to become more accomplished instead.'

'Fustian! I promise you that you are as pretty as any of them

– did you not look at yourself in the glass yesterday when you were wearing that delightful ensemble?'

'I looked passable Mama said, but nothing in comparison to Lydia or Kitty. I lack the necessary feminine curves and my hair is a nondescript colour – even my eyes would only be described as mud brown.'

The conversation was interrupted as two parlourmaids whisked in with their refreshments. Once they were private, Georgiana returned to the attack. 'You have lived in the shadow of your sisters for far too long, and Mrs Bennet has overlooked you. Dressed in more becoming gowns, and with your hair arranged differently, you will be amazed what a difference it will make.' Mary looked unconvinced. 'Please, allow me to take you in hand. We are of similar build and I have a dozen or more gowns that will look wonderful on you. Ellie, my maid, shall do your hair.'

By the time they had cleared the trays Mary was more relaxed and even smiled a time or two. The metamorphosis would not happen overnight, but Georgiana was determined to transform her new friend into a beautiful young lady before they left for London at the end of the month.

12

The weeks flew past and Georgiana grew closer to Mary, although there would always be a reserve between them as they were not as compatible as she and Kitty were. The newlyweds had spent the day at Pemberley and would remain to dine with them. This meant there was no necessity to change, so her dearest friend and she could remain in her apartment and talk.

The first topic of conversation was Mary. Kitty was astounded at the change in her sister. 'I cannot believe it, Georgiana dearest; I scarcely recognised my sister when I saw her. You have worked wonders. I am sure she will now enjoy the balls and parties and will be surrounded by eager suitors.'

'I do hope so. She did not seem particularly overjoyed when Lizzy explained Mary now had a substantial dowry.'

'Unfortunately my sibling seems determined not to enjoy life. However, I'm hopeful that once she is surrounded by gaiety and attends a few soirées and balls, she will change her mind. Is your brother to come with us when we leave the day after tomorrow?'

'Yes he will come with us, but is only staying until we are

launched into society. He is concerned that Lizzy might overtax herself if he is not here to keep an eye on her.' Georgiana was worried that there might not be a happy outcome. 'Although the babies are not expected until the beginning of July she is already so big I fear she might have them early. There would be little chance of the infants surviving if they arrived more than a week or two before their due time – at least that's what Jane has told me.'

'We must not worry about Lizzy, dearest, she is as strong as a horse, so she is always telling us, and as long as she takes care of herself, I am sure that the babies will stay where they should be for the required time.' Kitty sounded so certain, Georgiana smiled, perhaps she was being overanxious.

'Jane is blooming; being with child seems to suit them both.' Her friend had been remarkably reticent about the joys of being a wife. She had blushed and giggled when questioned and refused to reveal any secrets of the marriage bed, so there was no point in making further inquiries on that subject.

'Will you be happy if you are in the same condition so soon?'

Kitty's smile slipped a little. 'If I'm honest, I would much prefer not to start filling my nursery just yet. Adam and I are going on a belated wedding trip. Unfortunately we cannot go abroad, but he's taking me to the wilds of Scotland and that will be adventure enough.'

'Remember that I am getting married in September, and that you have nieces and nephews due in July. Surely you do not intend to miss any of these family occasions?'

'Of course I do not, you pea-goose, we shall leave immediately after your wedding. The weather does not deteriorate, even in Scotland, until the end of October so there will be ample time.'

They chatted away of inconsequential things until it was

time to join the others in the small drawing room. Fitzwilliam had dispensed with the custom of gathering in the Great Hall before dinner as he had no wish for his dearest wife to become chilled.

Another subject that had been avoided was the continued absence of Mrs Bennet. Fitzwilliam had heard from his men at Longbourn and discovered Lydia, her mother and husband had arrived safely. His spies would ensure that if any of them departed from this place, word would be sent immediately.

Mr Bennet was remarkably cheerful for a gentleman whose wife had abandoned him; however, he was resigned to returning to his marital home when they departed for Town. He had promised to return for another visit when the babies were due.

After a pleasant dinner, the party regrouped again in the small drawing room. Kitty was now included in the circle with Jane and Lizzy, whilst she and Mary, as unmarried girls, chose to sit apart. Not for the first time she wished that Jonathan was here with her; although she had already received two loving letters from him, she sorely missed him and was counting the days until he got leave to visit her.

'Georgiana, you are wool-gathering. I'm quite sure you did not hear my question.' Mary was staring at her crossly.

'You are quite correct; I do apologise for not paying attention. What did you ask me?'

Mary sighed loudly. 'I wish to know if you have already received invitations. Lizzy told me the house in Grosvenor Square is already opened and the staff in place, so surely any correspondence would have been forwarded to you here?'

'I have not thought to ask, Mary. Shall we do so now? I would much prefer to sit with the others than remain here on our own.' No sooner had she spoken than she realised this comment could be misconstrued. 'I do enjoy spending time with you, but...'

Too late – her companion was already on her feet, her lips tight, and her eyes unfriendly. 'I understand perfectly. I shall retire; I know when I am not wanted.'

Jane had seen her sister depart and called over. 'Dearest Georgiana, do not look so bothered by Mary's abrupt disappearance. Despite her improved appearance, she is still the same girl underneath – always quick to take offence when none has been intended.'

'I suggested that we come and join you, and she took this as a slight on her company. I had thought we'd become friends, but my thoughtless remark has set us back to the beginning.'

'You must ignore her when she is out of sorts; she will be recovered tomorrow. I was about to call you over anyway, I much prefer it when we all sit together,' Lizzy said with a smile. 'Never mind what convention dictates, we are not discussing anything unsuitable for unmarried young ladies.'

Kitty grabbed Georgiana's hand and pulled her down beside her on the daybed. 'Anyway, dearest, you will be married soon enough. I do hope that Mary allows herself to enjoy her time in London, for if she walks about as if she had swallowed a cup of vinegar she will not find herself a suitable match.'

'Good heavens, Kitty, we are not sending her to London in order to marry her off. However, you're right to be concerned – she can be as prickly as a hedgehog in company and I have no wish for anything to spoil your debut.'

This gave Georgiana the opportunity she had been waiting for to discuss what was expected of her while she was in London for two months or more. 'I know that you and Fitzwilliam want me to look around for someone more eligible than Jonathan; however, I can assure you I shall not be doing so. Like Kitty with

Adam, I knew the moment I set eyes on him that he was the gentleman for me. I care naught if a duke offers for my hand; I am already spoken for and have no intention of changing my mind.' There, she had said it at last.

Her sisters exchanged knowing glances and did not seem particularly surprised at her forceful statement. It was Lizzy who responded. 'Even Fitzwilliam has accepted the inevitable, my love. Neither of us would dream of separating you from the major if you are set on marrying him. The fact that he is without a fortune is immaterial to us; he is a good man, a gentleman, and he loves you to distraction.' She paused and glanced lovingly at her husband who was deep in conversation with the other gentlemen at the far end of the room.

'Indeed, your brother has written to Major Brownstone releasing him from his promise.'

'Promise? What promise is this?' Her heart thumped uncomfortably and she clenched her fists, fearing she would get an answer she did not wish to hear.

'Fitzwilliam only agreed to your engagement on the understanding that the major would release you if you found someone more to your liking. He had no choice, Georgiana, but to accept this proviso.'

She blinked back unwanted tears. 'I cannot believe what you're telling me, Lizzy; how could Jonathan have agreed? I knew about this but did not for a moment believe the arrangement to be genuine. He must secretly wish to be free of me; he would never have done so otherwise.' She scrambled to her feet, mumbled her goodbyes, and fled to the safety of her apartment.

* * *

'Lizzy dearest, you must not upset yourself. You know it is bad for ladies in your condition to become distressed. Shall I go after her?' Jane hesitated and then continued. 'Actually, as I was not privy to this secret, I do not think I can be of much use in reassuring Georgiana.'

Lizzy watched Georgiana run out, knowing it was she who should go after her, but she was too fatigued to get to her feet. Kitty must go, but her sister was looking shocked. 'Please, Kitty, do not take umbrage. I cannot cope with so much upset in one evening.' Her eyes filled and she rummaged for her handkerchief in her reticule. Since she had been with child she was a veritable watering pot.

Then Fitzwilliam was beside her, looking none too pleased. 'What in heaven's name is going on down here? First Mary runs away and then Georgiana, and now I find you in tears, Lizzy.'

'I do not blame Georgiana for being distressed; she has just heard the most unsettling news. I can hardly credit that you told the major he could only become betrothed to your sister if he promised to stand aside if she had a better offer. That is quite outrageous, Mr Darcy. I am shocked to the marrow.' Kitty stood up and immediately Adam was at her side.

'I have the headache, Adam. Would you mind very much if we left early?' He looked from one to the other and understood immediately there was something untoward going on, but he refrained from interfering.

He bowed to Fitzwilliam and herself. 'Thank you for a delightful day, Lizzy. I shall take Kitty home now, but we will see you the day after tomorrow when we collect Georgiana and Mary.'

With his arm around her sister's waist he led her away. Ignoring Jane and Bingley who were watching anxiously,

Fitzwilliam sat next to her on the daybed and took her hands in his. 'Sweetheart, how in tarnation has it come to this?'

She sniffed and blew her nose whilst she gathered her scattered wits. 'I fear it was entirely my fault. I blurted it out without thinking. Georgiana had thought the arrangement false, and her realisation that it wasn't has caused this upset.

'My head is filled with feathers at the moment; I'm not my usual self. Georgiana thinks the major has betrayed her by agreeing, and Kitty blames us for suggesting it. I've no idea what nonsense sent Mary scampering off.'

'Too late to recant, my love, we must just pray that Georgiana is willing to listen to us when she has calmed down. I wish Kitty had followed and spoken to my sister instead of leaving so abruptly.'

'I believe Kitty would have made matters worse. I should have gone myself but found I didn't have the energy. Papa is coming over; I think it best if we keep this matter private.' She looked at Jane and Bingley, who nodded quickly.

'I have been thinking about my return to Longbourn and have decided I shall remain here instead. Mrs Bennet still has the Wickhams living there; until they leave I have no wish to return. I do not like the notion of you being without Darcy when he goes to London,' Papa said firmly.

'You should write to Mama and tell her that Lydia and Wickham must leave immediately. It is not right that you are kept from your own home by those two. Although it would be delightful to have you here, remember that I have Jane and Bingley as company, and Fitzwilliam will be away for less than a sennight.'

Her father shook his head. 'After the threats they made, I think it better if we know where they are. Do you not agree with me, Darcy?'

'You are right, Mr Bennet. Lizzy and I are convinced they can do Georgiana no harm, but it is sensible to be cautious where they are concerned. Remain at Pemberley – you are welcome to do so for as long as you wish.'

Mr Bennet retired, meaning they could converse freely. 'I am as surprised as the girls that Major Brownstone agreed to such a plan. Somehow I cannot see him standing aside for another gentleman. He is besotted with Georgiana,' Jane said and looked at Bingley for confirmation. Her husband nodded.

'You are right, dearest Jane, even Adam says so and he is the fellow's closest friend. Even without the letter you have sent rescinding your instructions, Darcy, I shouldn't be surprised if the major appears in London at the earliest opportunity. His presence there will make it very clear to all concerned that he is Georgiana's future husband.'

'I do hope you're right, Bingley. With the major and Adam watching over her, I am certain Georgiana will be safe, even if that wretched man does attempt to cause difficulties.' Lizzy was ready to retire. 'Fitzwilliam, would you kindly assist me to my feet? I must bid you goodnight, Jane, Bingley; there has been too much excitement for me.'

It was not yet nine o'clock but they all decided to retire. Doubtless the staff would be delighted at having the remainder of the evening free. With Fitzwilliam's arm to support her, Lizzy was able to negotiate the endless corridors and ascend the Grand Staircase.

'I believe it might be sensible to move downstairs for the remainder of my confinement. Would you mind very much if we did that?'

'I was about to suggest it myself, Lizzy, but knowing how independent you are I hesitated to do so. The only drawback to this plan, as far as I can see, is that we will no longer have the use of the bathing room.'

Lizzy laughed. 'My darling, I have not been able to use the bath for several weeks so that will be no loss to me. I know I should not complain about my condition, but I can tell you that I am already finding this pregnancy a sore trial and will be delighted when our babies are born.'

'I know it has been difficult for you, sweetheart, but the longer your pregnancy continues the better it will be for our children.'

She was obliged to pause and catch her breath and leaned against him whilst she did so. Despite her ungainly size he was as loving and supportive as he had always been. She sighed noisily. 'And that's another thing, dearest, I miss the intimacy of the marriage bed and cannot wait to resume our lovemaking.'

His response was immediate. He cupped her face and tilted her head to receive his hard and passionate kiss. Several delightful minutes later he raised his head. 'As I am sure you are aware, my love, I find you desirable even though you are the size of a beached whale.'

* * *

Georgiana heard them laughing and this fuelled her anger. How dare they treat her as if she was a child without the ability to make her own decisions? It would serve all of them right if she did find someone else and broke off the engagement.

Then she gulped back a sob. However angry she was with Jonathan she would never jilt him. As her misery abated she came up with a scheme that would not only be fun to execute but also teach Jonathan, her interfering brother, and Lizzy, a well-deserved lesson.

As Jonathan had yet to give her a betrothal ring, her left hand would be ringless. She would pretend to be a debutante in search of an eligible bachelor. She would dance with anyone who asked, flutter her eyelids and her fan and be the epitome of a silly young thing experiencing her first Season.

This was something she would not contemplate if Jonathan was to accompany her, but he would be safely with his regiment and could have nothing to say on the matter. Anyway, it would serve him right if he did hear about her outrageous behaviour; after all he had been the one to cast doubts on their future union by agreeing to such a hurtful and stupid arrangement.

Tomorrow the baggage cart, and both her dresser and the one assigned to Mary, would leave for Town. The next day she would depart and the Darcy carriage would transport her and Mary to the Old Rectory and there Kitty and Adam would join them.

Her brother had changed his mind about accompanying them; he intended to come to London only for her ball. He did not wish to leave Lizzy for any longer than a week.

The journey would be long and tedious, and involve three overnight stops, but she was well used to travelling and it held no fears for her. During this time she must keep her plan a secret, pretend that she had recovered from her upset, and behave with her usual decorum and propriety.

She giggled into her pillow at the thought of behaving badly. All her life she had been a dutiful young lady and she could not wait to begin her masquerade.

13

The staff at Grosvenor Square had the house pristine and Georgiana greeted the butler and housekeeper by name – after all they had known her since she was a small girl.

'I hope the baggage carts arrived safely yesterday, Robinson?'

The butler bowed. 'Everything is as it should be, Miss Darcy. Your apartment is prepared and your trunks are unpacked.'

Watkins – who was housekeeper here – curtsied, making her stiff, bombazine gown crackle. 'I have put Miss Bennet in the guest wing with Mr and Mrs King. If you would prefer her to be accommodated elsewhere, that can be arranged in an instant.'

Mary had been remarkably taciturn on the long journey from Derbyshire and Georgiana feared the progress they had made in becoming friends was lost. She turned to her companion. 'I should love to have you next door, but will leave the decision to you, Miss Bennet.'

Surprisingly, the girl almost smiled. 'I would love to be next to you, Miss Darcy, and not in the guest wing, if that is not too much trouble.'

The housekeeper nodded and snapped her fingers. Immediately a waiting footman whisked away to set things in motion. 'Your chamber will be ready within a quarter of an hour, Miss Bennet. If you would care to wait in the drawing room I shall have a tray sent to you directly.'

Kitty and Adam, who had stopped to admire the surroundings, now arrived in the commodious entrance hall. 'Did I hear mention of refreshments? I'm half dead with hunger and thirst – it is an age since we ate – and what we had was hardly substantial.' Kitty danced into the centre of the space and spun around like a child. 'I love this house; I never thought to spend time in Town and certainly not in such a splendid place as this.'

Her husband stopped her mad gyrations by lifting her from the floor and holding her for a brief moment against his chest. Georgiana's eyes filled when she saw how much love there was between them. She prayed that her own relationship would be as joyous.

'Kitty, sweetheart, enough of this silliness. You are a sedate married woman now, and must behave accordingly.' His words were stern but his eyes were smiling and Kitty poked out her tongue in response. What the watching staff thought of this performance Georgiana had no idea, but she loved to see them so happy and relaxed in each other's company.

'Watkins, kindly send refreshments to the drawing room immediately. We shall go to our rooms later.'

The four of them hurried into the drawing room. This was filled with early April sunshine and looking particularly attractive. The house was much warmer than Pemberley, and far more convenient, and if it wasn't for the noxious smells and smoke of London, it would be a delightful place to live.

'I wonder what invitations have arrived for us; I see there are a substantial number of them on the silver salver on the side table over there.' Georgiana fetched the pile of crisp, white cards, but instead of reading them all herself, she divided the invitations between them. 'There must be more than a score. We shall sort them out and decide which we will attend. There are bound to be some where the dates clash.'

By the time invitations had been sorted into those that they would attend in full, those that they might drop into, and those that they would politely refuse, the rattle of crockery heralded the arrival of the eagerly awaited refreshments.

'There must be some replies to the invitations to our ball, Kitty. Can you see them anywhere?'

'I shall look. Fortunately this chamber is not as large as any at Pemberley and it should not take me too long.'

Mary joined her in the search. 'This house is very like Netherfield, is it not? I prefer a place where I can find my way about without being in need of a map.'

Georgiana exchanged a smile with Adam, both pleased that Mary was finally becoming less prickly and more relaxed. The missing replies were soon discovered and, as expected, they were all acceptances. This was the first ball to be held at the Darcy house in living memory and the *ton* would all be curious to see the interior of the building.

Of course there had been private parties, musical evenings and so on, but only members of a select group would have been included in these invitations. There were over two hundred guests invited to the ball, which was to be held at the end of April, a little over three weeks away. No doubt preparations were already in hand below stairs.

* * *

Georgiana woke to the sound of rain beating against the windowpanes. Botheration! They could hardly visit the menagerie at the Tower in such a deluge. Perhaps braver folk would still be prepared to make morning calls, and this would mean that the afternoon would pass more quickly.

Ellie appeared with her morning chocolate and sweet rolls. 'Good morning, miss, what would you like me to lay out for you? I fear you will not be able to walk as you planned.'

'I shall leave the choice to you, Ellie – something that is acceptable if the weather improves and we are able to venture out.'

Her morning ablutions were cursory as she had had the luxury of a bath in front of the fire in the dressing room before she had retired last night. Dressed in a simple but elegant gown of cambric, in a delightful shade of damask-rose, she was ready and eager to visit next door and see if Mary was ready to go downstairs for breakfast.

She glanced at the tall-case clock that ticked loudly in the corner of her private sitting room. The time had sped past, it was almost ten o'clock. She was tardy; everyone would be in the breakfast parlour already. There was little point in calling for her neighbour as Mary would already have gone down.

She dashed through the house revelling in the unaccustomed warmth – even the corridors and passageways were pleasant. There was no necessity for a spencer or a wrap when living here.

The door to the breakfast room stood open and she could hear voices inside. She dashed through the door, expecting to see all three of her guests seated around the table, but only Kitty and Adam were there. 'Has Mary already breakfasted?'

Kitty waved her fork in the air. 'Good morning, dearest Georgiana, and no, my sister has not come down yet.'

'I beg your pardon, good morning, Kitty and Adam. Kindly excuse me, I must go back and fetch Mary.'

She gathered her skirts and raced through the house, relieved she did not meet any members of staff in her mad dash. It was fortunate that servants were trained not to be seen upstairs unless on an errand for the family.

Breathless and somewhat red in the face, she skidded to a halt outside Mary's sitting room door. She knocked loudly and immediately there were running footsteps and the door flew open.

'Thank goodness, I thought I was forgotten. I am sharp-set and desperate for my breakfast.' Mary gave her the first genuine smile she had seen. 'I should have said good morning, but I am sure you will forgive me.'

'I was so late that I assumed you had gone down without me. When I discovered this not to be the case I came back at once, hence my dishevelled appearance and shortness of breath.' Georgiana giggled and grabbed Mary's hand. 'Pick up your skirts, sister; we shall run all the way back. Excellent exercise and will sharpen our appetites wonderfully.'

They erupted into the breakfast parlour, causing Adam to slop his coffee onto his plate and say something reprehensible. Amidst much laughter and apologies all round she and Mary piled their plates and joined the other two at the table.

'The weather is appalling today, ladies, so have you any suggestions as to what we might do instead of traipsing around the menagerie?'

Kitty spoke up immediately. 'Hatchards – I have always wished to visit – one cannot have too many books.'

He grinned. 'My love, I believe I would prefer to be soaked to the skin at the menagerie. I can think of nothing worse than escorting three young ladies to a bookshop full of romantic nonsense and other chattering females.'

'It will be perfectly acceptable, Adam, for us to go without a male escort. Indeed, we do not even need to take our maids with us.' Georgiana knew this to be true as her governess had explained what was acceptable for a young lady to do without a gentleman in attendance.

His look of relief was comical. Kitty pouted and tilted her head to one side. 'You are excused this time, husband, but be very sure I shall think of something for you to do with us that you will find equally unpalatable.'

'I am, as always, at your service, my love. However, as I am excused duty this morning I shall take the opportunity to conduct some business of my own.' He put down his napkin and stood up. 'Are we to make calls this afternoon?'

'There were more than a dozen cards left yesterday saying they would return this afternoon to welcome us to London,' Georgiana told him.

'In which case, ladies, I shall see you later.' He strolled to the door and with a casual wave was gone.

'I have made morning calls with Mama, and been in to receive them in return. However, at Longbourn we never had more than two visitors at one time, did we, Kitty?'

'There will be a procession of callers, Mary, and no doubt there will be several young gentlemen dragged along so that they may be introduced to us.'

'Why should anyone wish to be introduced to me? Indeed, Georgiana, as you are already spoken for, I cannot see they will gain any benefit from coming.'

'Mary, dearest, have you not looked at yourself in the glass today? With your hair dressed so prettily and in that delightful ensemble you will be in high demand. And don't forget that you are now an eligible heiress – the two things combined will mean that Adam will be kept busy vetting your suitors.'

If Georgiana had suggested Mary was a devil worshipper she could not have had a more shocked response. She scrambled to her feet and was about to run away but Kitty was quicker and got to the door before her.

'Don't be a pea-goose, there is nothing to be afraid of. No one is going to force you into matrimony if you have no wish to do so. You are here to have fun, to dance and enjoy yourself at parties and routs and musicales.' Kitty took her sister's elbow and gently led her back and positioned her in front of the small mirror that hung above the sideboard. 'Look at yourself. What do you see?'

Georgiana joined them and slipped her arm around Mary's waist. 'We see a lovely young lady, elegant and beautifully gowned, and someone who will be the belle of the ball.'

'I do not see what you both see, but I am forced to agree my appearance is much improved. I cannot promise to enjoy myself, but I will certainly try.'

'We can ask no more than that of you, Mary, but I give you my word you will definitely enjoy some of the things you experience. I am not overfond of musicales – far too often the performers are sadly lacking in talent.' Georgiana released her hold. 'There, we are now all in agreement. The carriage will be here in a quarter of an hour; we must hurry and get ready.'

* * *

Lizzy collected the three letters that had arrived that morning. One was for her father, one for Fitzwilliam and the other for herself. Her heart plummeted as she recognised the writing. The missive was from Mama. There must be something dreadfully wrong for her parent to communicate when there was such bad feeling between them.

She decided to find somewhere private and comfortable to sit down before she opened it – if it were to be bad news she was not sure, in her enfeebled state, that she would be able to remain upright. Fitzwilliam was busy with his estate manager. Jane and Bingley were overseeing the improvements to their new home next door in the east wing, so the small drawing room would be free.

Once she was comfortably settled on the *chaise longue* she broke open the wax seal and with shaking fingers smoothed out the paper. Immediately she saw it had been written several days ago.

> *My dear Elizabeth,*
>
> *I know that we are not on the best of terms at present, but I fear something so dreadful has occurred at Longbourn that I had no option but to write to you. I have also written to Mr Bennet, but I fear he will be able to do nothing. I should really have communicated with Mr Darcy, but he puts me in such a tremble when he is looking at me that I cannot bring myself to do so.*
>
> *As you know Lydia and Wickham came with me to Longbourn and have remained here these past few weeks. I cannot tell you how my opinion has changed, how deceived I was in him, how Lydia has become another person, someone I do not recognise as my dearest daughter.*

Lizzy wished her mother would get to the point, but she wrote as she spoke and whatever news she had was well-disguised within the rambling. There was no point in skipping to the bottom; she might well miss the salient points by so doing. With a sigh of exasperation she continued to read:

> *I know you will be wondering what it is your sister and her wretched husband have done that has so discommoded me. I do wish dear Mr Bennet was here to advise me – I am at a loss to know what to do for the best, which is why I have written to you in the hope that you will pass on this dire information to Mr Darcy.*
>
> *Throughout the time the two of them were with me they did nothing but complain and criticise our family and they were particularly unkind about Georgiana and Major Brownstone. At first I let them rant and rail, but after a week or so I became tired of hearing so much unpleasantness. I began to reprimand Lydia and she did not take kindly to this.*
>
> *Before I knew it they turned on me. I too was blamed for having them evicted from Pemberley. I had nothing whatsoever to do with this and took their side against you and Mr Darcy. My staff became reluctant to serve them and there were reports of Wickham meeting up with ne'er-do-wells in the local hostelry.*
>
> *Then when I got up this morning they had gone, taking the carriage and all the silver and valuables as well. I had never thought my Lydia could treat me so badly or that Wickham was a thief.*

At last – now they were coming to the nub of the matter. Lizzy was not surprised that Wickham and Lydia had shown their true colours, but for them to have stolen from Longbourn beggared belief. Without a carriage Mama was marooned in Hertfordshire and could not return to Derbyshire. Unfortunately there was worse to come:

Mr Bennet's man of business arrived soon after they departed with the most dreadful news. Someone in Meryton overheard Wickham talking and immediately fetched this information to Longbourn. Wickham and Lydia intend to go to London and cause trouble for Georgiana. When they sell the silver and other items they will be in funds, and they have taken these local villains with them.

Lizzy clutched the paper to her chest. For a moment she was unable to breathe, but then common sense reasserted itself. If Papa had received the same news he would already be on his way to speak to her, but she must send a footman to fetch Fitzwilliam immediately. Even if he travelled post, he could not reach London in less than two days and this letter had taken five to reach them. Would he be in time to save Georgiana from disaster?

14

Georgiana was on her own perusing the latest arrivals at the bookshop when she saw a familiar figure approaching. 'Lady Rawlings, I did not know you were to be in London this year. I am pleased to see you again.' Georgiana sincerely hoped Mr Rawlings had not accompanied his mother.

'My dear Miss Darcy, what a surprise to see you here in Hatchards. Such dreadful weather; my dear girls refused to accompany me. Will you be at the Fairfax ball tomorrow?'

'We will, Lady Rawlings, no doubt we shall meet with you there. If you would excuse me, Mrs King and Miss Bennet are waiting at the door so the carriage must have come for us.'

She hurried away, relieved that Lady Rawlings had not mentioned the Darcy ball, or the fact that there had been no invitation sent to them. Fitzwilliam had been adamant in his decision that these people should not attend after Mr Rawlings' involvement with Wickham.

Kitty greeted her with enthusiasm. 'There you are at last; we had quite thought you lost forever amongst the books. See, the carriage is just coming and we must not let the poor horses stand in this torrential rain.'

As soon as the vehicle trundled to a halt Georgiana led the rush to scramble in before they were soaked to the skin. Once inside, with the steps safely up and the door closed tight, she was a little warmer.

'Look, Kitty, your bonnet is dripping,' Mary commented.

Then Kitty squealed with dismay. 'My cherries are bleeding!' She held up a red-stained glove to prove the point. 'I must look as if I have been in a dreadful accident. Is my face covered in streaks as well?'

'Oh dear, you must remove your bonnet, Kitty, or it will ruin your pelisse,' Georgiana said trying not to laugh.

Even Mary joined in and soon all of them were giggling. Kitty's face was an interesting shade of pink and the guilty bonnet had been tossed to the floor of the carriage where she poked at it with her foot in disgust.

'Lizzy warned me not to put them on, but I didn't listen. I am very fond of this bonnet and I fear it is past redemption.'

'I think I could do something with it, Kitty; do not despair. It would be a shame to throw it away when it has been made to match your ensemble so perfectly.' Mary leaned down and was about to pick up the sodden object when both Georgiana and Kitty restrained her.

'Don't touch it, Mary, there is no point in both of us having ruined gloves. A footman can take it in for us and I shall give it to Annie to dry. When it is safe to handle I shall get her to bring it to you.' Kitty smiled at her sister and Mary settled back without argument.

Georgiana was unsure whether she should mention that she had met Lady Rawlings in the bookshop. She had no wish to remind her friends of the unpleasantness that had taken place at Kitty's wedding. Perhaps in this case, silence was golden.

The afternoon was filled with morning callers and Georgiana was amused by how many young gentlemen had been dragged along to what was essentially a ladies' outing.

The rule was that no visitor remained above a quarter of an hour, and this was scrupulously adhered to by her guests. Adam stood behind Kitty's chair, glowering at any gentleman who dared to look in her direction, and she envied her friend for having his protection. She wished, not for the first time, that Jonathan was free to be with her and not duty-bound to fight for King and Country.

Surprisingly Mary had become quite animated and she received several admiring looks from hopeful gentlemen. Georgiana decided that if she could not have Jonathan with her, then she would make a push to find Mary a suitable husband.

It wasn't until she was snuggling beneath the comforter that night that she recalled her earlier vow to misbehave and flirt outrageously with any gentleman who showed an interest. Perhaps this was not such a good idea – not only would it be unpleasant for her companions, it would also be unfair to those she singled out.

No, she must put aside this silly notion and behave as she always did, with the utmost decorum and good manners. They all had new ball gowns to wear tomorrow night to the come-out ball for Lady Serena Fairfax – Kitty, as a married woman, was now able to wear bright colours and had selected a dashing confection in emerald green. Mary would be wearing palest gold, with a sparkling sarcenet overskirt, and golden beading around the hem and neckline.

Georgiana sighed. She had three new gowns. Tomorrow she intended to wear the white silk with the silver sparkles. The most beautiful she was keeping for her own ball; she sent up a little prayer to the Almighty that her beloved might be able to attend and see her in her finery.

* * *

Fortunately, by eight o'clock the next evening, when they were to leave for the ball, the relentless rain had eased and although the cobbles were wet and the pavements slippery, there was no risk that they would be obliged to huddle beneath umbrellas as they made their way into the venue.

Georgiana swirled her evening cloak around her shoulders and tied the bow before carefully arranging the hood over her expertly coiffured hair. Ellie was to accompany them, and she would take her work basket and be ready to repair any damage that might occur. She would also have a slipper bag containing fresh pairs, for if one danced a lot one's slippers would be quite ruined before the evening was over. No party was allowed more than one attendant at these occasions and it had been decided that her own maid should be the one to come.

Kitty had joined her in her sitting room just before they left and she had shared her plans for Mary with her. 'I think that a splendid idea, dearest Georgiana. Between us we will find a fine selection of suitable gentlemen from which Mary can choose. I have told Adam that I intend to dance as often as I wish. He was not impressed with my decision, but has grudgingly agreed as long as he is introduced to my partners first.'

'We must hope that whoever asks us is someone we will enjoy spending time with. It would be so much simpler if we were allowed to refuse a gentleman we did not like the look of. I think it a ridiculous rule that a young lady must either dance with anyone who asks, or not get up for that dance at all.'

There was a polite tap on the door and Mary entered. 'You look so beautiful; that dress is a triumph. You will be the centre of attention tonight, I'm quite sure it.' Kitty rushed across and embraced her sister, who looked thoroughly embarrassed by the praise.

'I agree most wholeheartedly, Mary. Tonight we will conquer the *ton*. There will be no other trio of young ladies as beautiful.'

A more vigorous knock on the door heralded the arrival of Adam. He too was struck dumb for a moment as he viewed them in their finery. 'A bevy of beauties, and I have the impossible task of keeping you all safe from importunate and undesirable young men.' He smiled and offered his arm to Kitty. 'I thank the good Lord that at least you already have a ring on your finger and there's no danger of you being swept off your feet.'

'I can assure you, sir, that you have no worry on my score either. I am affianced to Jonathan and there is no danger of my being swept anywhere by anyone.'

She tucked her hand through Mary's arm and followed on behind Adam and Kitty. Mary whispered to her, 'You will stay with me, won't you, Georgiana? Although I have attended many balls at the Assembly Rooms at Meryton, I have never been to such a prestigious occasion. Neither have I been obliged to meet so many strangers in one evening.'

'You will be perfectly splendid, Mary, and if you do not like the look of someone then Adam shall merely have to scowl at him and he will vanish with his tail between his legs. Surely you went to the Netherfield ball? Was that not a grand occasion too?'

'Indeed it was, but I remained in the background and danced with no one. I am accustomed to being a wallflower; I will find it quite alarming if you are correct in your assumptions.'

There was no further opportunity for private conversation and Georgiana hoped that Mary would not allow her natural reserve to spoil her evening. This was the first important event in the social calendar and even though the journey was a scant mile from Grosvenor Square, she was resigned to being in the carriage for an hour or more. Their vehicle would join a line of like-minded ones and they would creep forward one by one in a long queue until they finally arrived at the red carpet and could disembark.

Eventually it was their turn and two immaculately clad footmen opened the door, let down the steps and Kitty was handed out. Mary followed and she came last. She supposed she should have gone before Mary, but such niceties did not bother her.

'It is very exciting, Kitty. The flambeaux make everything look mysterious. I believe I am actually looking forward to this event. There will be so many other guests I should be able to hide behind a pillar and not be noticed, if I so wish.' Mary was gripping her arm as if it were a lifeline.

'You will do no such thing. Kitty and I will not let you hide. You will dance as often as we do and I insist that you enjoy it.'

It took an interminable time to creep up the wide staircase to the reception rooms on the first floor where they were to be greeted by their host and hostess and their daughter. The ladies' retiring rooms were on the ground floor and Ellie had taken their reticules and cloaks away with her and would wait, along with others like her, to offer assistance if required.

Georgiana was aware they were attracting a deal of attention and she could not decide whether it was the fact that they were escorted by the handsomest man in the room, or that all three of them looked like diamonds of the first water. Her engagement was still not common knowledge. Friends and close acquaintances were aware of her attachment, but nobody here would be.

Adam guided them to a small group of spindly gilt chairs placed at one side of the splendid ballroom. 'I think this is a perfect place for us. I can stand behind you and scare off anyone unsuitable before they get the chance to approach. Kitty sweetheart, we shall dance when Mary and Georgiana are safely partnered.'

'Why is everyone looking at us, Georgiana?' Mary asked quietly.

'It is because we are so beautiful tonight. I don't suppose the dancing will commence until everybody is here, for the Fairfax family must remain to greet all the guests.'

Adam, from his great height, was able to see across the crowd into the spacious area outside the room. 'Devil take it! Excuse me, ladies, I have business to attend to. You will all remain where you are until I return.' He strode away, a grim expression on his face.

Kitty pointed to the chair she had been about to sit on. 'I believe that if I stood on that I could see what has upset him.'

'No, you must not do that. It will draw unwanted attention to ourselves,' Georgiana said.

'Shall we sit down? There is a group of determined-looking ladies approaching our chairs.' Mary did as she suggested and they followed suit.

The orchestra continued to play and because they were almost underneath the gallery upon which they stood, it made conversation all but impossible unless one was prepared to shout. Georgiana flicked open her fan and busied herself with this in the hope it would calm her nerves; she had an awful sinking feeling that somehow Wickham and Lydia had obtained invitations and were about to carry out their threats.

Kitty touched her hand and she was obliged to face her. 'What is wrong, dearest? You have gone as pale as a sheet. Surely you do not think that wretched man has managed to inveigle an entrance here?'

'I do. I cannot think of anything else that could have sent Adam away in such fury. I don't feel at all well; I wish I had not come here tonight. In fact, I wish I had stayed at home in Derbyshire.'

She glanced round to see that Mary was no longer in her chair, but she had had the foresight to place her fan on the seat, indicating it was taken.

'Mary must have gone to find out what is happening; I had not thought she had the courage to venture through the crowds on her own.'

'Pemberley and you, dearest Georgiana, have begun to work their magic on my sister. Not only has her appearance changed but also her character. There is nothing we can do about it. We must not appear discomfited but smile and nod as if we are delighted to be here.'

As the guests drifted past in clouds of perfume and silk Georgiana did as she was bid, but with each minute that passed her anxiety increased. Then Mary was back and seated between them.

'There is nothing to worry about. Mr King saw Sir Matthew and Lady Rawlings arriving with their family. Mr Rawlings was with them and it was he who caused Adam to be cross.'

Kitty hugged her sister, ignoring the raised eyebrows from those around them. Such open displays of affection were frowned upon in public. 'Thank you for telling us. Now you can relax, Georgiana. Mr Rawlings is no threat to you. He is a silly young gentleman but perfectly harmless.'

The crowd milling about at the edges of the dance floor

parted and Adam marched through looking his usual self again. 'No doubt Mary has informed you why I was obliged to leave you unattended, ladies. I was unhappy that Rawlings should be here; any friend of Wickham is no friend of mine.' He resumed his position behind the chairs before continuing. 'I had a quiet word with him and he knows what to expect if he does anything to offend.'

'Thank you, sir, for your prompt action. I just hope he does not decide to ask me to dance, for I would not be comfortable doing so.'

'Sir Matthew spoke to me as well, my dear. He assured me that his son's connection to Wickham has been severed and that young Rawlings has no wish to have any further association with him or his wife.'

'Listen, the music has stopped. The dancing must be about to begin. Goodness me! There appears to be a crowd of young gentlemen heading our way with Lady Fairfax at their head.'

There followed a flurry of introductions and Adam had no opportunity to scrutinise the gentlemen introduced to her. Georgiana remembered none of the names and accepted an invitation to stand up in the first set with the least noisy of the group.

Lord Fairfax led his daughter onto the floor and immediately there was a surge from those waiting to dance and she had no opportunity to see with whom Mary had gone. She was whisked to the end of the ballroom and joined the line of ladies facing their partners. This was to be a country dance, which was fortunate as the steps were simple and she was unlikely to disgrace herself.

Her partner was pleasant enough, and she nodded, smiled and made appropriate replies when necessary, but she did not accept his request to dance again.

A succession of partners followed, none of them remarkable, but none of them stepped on her toes or caused her any embarrassment. She was delighted to note that Mary danced as often as she did and as the evening wore on her new friend began to look as if she was actually enjoying herself.

By the time the supper dance was called she had quite worn through her slippers. 'Adam, I must go to the retiring room. I have no wish to dance this time as I should then be obliged to accompany my partner whilst we eat. I might be gone a little while, so do not worry if the dance is ended before I return.'

Adam nodded. 'Do you wish me to accompany you? Are you sure you will be able to find your way back from the room you require?'

Kitty was tapping her foot, impatient to get back on the dance floor, having sat out for the previous dance. Mary was already being led out to make up the four couples necessary for a quadrille.

'There is no need, thank you, Adam; I shall be perfectly well. I know the room is downstairs, and I'm quite capable of asking a servant for directions if I cannot find it. Hopefully, if I go before the end of this dance, there will be less of a crush downstairs.'

The area outside the ballroom was quite busy, but fortunately not so many people as to be intimidating. No doubt those gentlemen and ladies who did not dance had taken their places in the rooms set aside for playing cards and everyone else was in the ballroom.

She held up the skirt of her gown and ran lightly down the staircase. At the bottom she was immediately approached by a parlourmaid who led her to the chamber she required.

Ellie was sent for and Georgiana changed her slippers, used the facilities, and was ready to return. As she stepped out into the corridor she could hear the strains of the music drifting down from upstairs. At least she would be in time to join her party for supper.

As she reached the vestibule she came face to face with Mr Rawlings. He bowed formally giving her no option but to respond. 'Good evening, Miss Darcy, I am delighted to be able to speak to you. I wish to offer my sincere and heartfelt apologies for bringing that villain, Wickham, to your home. I was quite misled by him. I had no idea he was a rogue.'

He sounded so contrite and his expression was sincere. 'In which case, sir, I accept your apology. That has put the matter behind us. Are you here for the Season or just here for this occasion?'

'My father has opened the town house and we are here for the duration. We are to hold a ball for my sisters. It is to be their come-out, but it will not be until the end of May. I hope that you will be able to attend.'

'I'm sure that if we have not already accepted an invitation for an event on the same night, we shall be pleased to come. I believe the music has stopped. I must hurry or I might fail to find my party in the rush to the supper room.'

'Mama and my sisters intend to call tomorrow afternoon. Would you object if I accompanied them?'

He had asked so charmingly, how could she refuse? He offered his arm with a friendly smile. 'Allow me to escort you, Miss Darcy. I give you my word as a gentleman you will not miss your supper.'

True to his word Mr Rawlings took her directly to the table reserved for their group. She had expected him to linger, waiting for an invitation to join them, but he half-bowed and strolled away to join his family at the far side of the room.

Adam watched him go. 'Where did you find him, Georgiana? I hope he did nothing to upset you.'

'Nothing at all I do assure you. He apologised most handsomely for his part in bringing that man to Pemberley and invited us to his sisters' ball. I accepted his invitation on the proviso that we are not already promised elsewhere.'

Kitty laughed. 'Well done, now we can refuse without giving offence if we decide we don't wish to go. Although I can see no reason why we should not attend. Sir Matthew and Lady Rawlings and their daughters are perfectly pleasant and are neighbours of ours, are they not?'

As Georgiana climbed into bed in the small hours she remembered she had not mentioned that Mrs Rawlings was intending to make a call. Adam could hardly object to that; after all there would be dozens of people in and out all afternoon.

15

Jonathan arrived at Grosvenor Square mid-morning. He had travelled post from the barracks at Colchester, deciding the exorbitant cost was worth it as he only had five days' leave of absence. Hopefully Georgiana would be in and not gallivanting around London.

His valise was damned heavy and he had been obliged to carry it for more than a mile from the coaching inn he had arrived at. Having already spent a month's wages on the journey he had no intention of wasting any further blunt on the unnecessary extravagance of hiring a jarvey.

Although there was a substantial sum invested in the funds, his prize money, he had not as yet dipped into this. If he wanted to keep up with the cream of society then he had better visit his bankers forthwith. It was fortunate he could appear in his dress uniform and not be obliged to purchase an evening rig and fancy slippers.

He strode to the front door and hammered on it. It was instantly thrown open; he had expected to be quizzed as to his identity, but the footman merely bowed and stepped aside to allow him to come in.

'Major Brownstone, the ladies are in the drawing room but Mr King has gone out.'

How the devil did a servant know his identity? He had said no word of his coming, so was not expected. He nodded his thanks and waited to be directed to the drawing room. The young man held out a hand for his things and Jonathan handed them over.

'This way, if you please, sir. A room will be prepared for you immediately. Do you wish for any refreshments to be sent?'

'Coffee, if there is any, will be sufficient.' He knew better than to thank a member of staff.

The footman knocked on the door and opened it with a flourish. 'Ladies, Major Brownstone.'

Jonathan walked in to a chorus of excited exclamations. Georgiana, looking delightful in a russet gown with gold embellishments, flung down the book she was reading and ran towards him.

'Jonathan, we were just talking about you. I cannot tell you how pleased I am to see you.'

He opened his arms and she threw herself into them. Ignoring the interested duo sitting by the fire he pulled his beloved closer and when she tilted her face he could not resist and covered her mouth with his. His heart pounded and he wanted to pick her up and find somewhere private so he could make love to her. Reluctantly he raised his head and stared down into her beautiful eyes.

'My darling girl, I had not thought to receive such a wonderful reception. I have arrived quite unannounced and have no wish to be in the way.'

'I did not enjoy myself at all last night without you to dance with. We are at home this afternoon, and this evening we attend a supper party somewhere or other.'

'I shall be delighted to escort you, my love.' He now turned to greet Kitty and Miss Bennet. 'Kitty, married life agrees with you, you are looking quite radiant. Miss Bennet, you too are looking splendid. Being in Town obviously suits you.'

In fact he had been confused as to whom the third attractive young lady was, but then realised it was Miss Bennet, quite transformed. What a difference a smiling countenance and a pretty gown had made to her appearance.

A short while later Adam joined them and his friend appeared equally pleased to see him. 'I need to speak to you, Jonathan. Shall we escape to the billiard room whilst the ladies are examining the latest fashion plates?'

There was no need for him to make his apologies as Georgiana smiled and waved him away. Once comfortably ensconced in the billiard room, and sitting on comfortable armchairs in front of the roaring fire, he waited for his friend to explain what was amiss.

'Why are you here? Have you heard something to bring you in such a rush to London?'

'I've heard nothing untoward from Georgiana. I am here because I have chosen to ignore the agreement I made with Darcy. I intend to make it known to all and sundry that Georgiana is spoken for, that we are betrothed and intend to get married at the end of the summer.'

'I thought the arrangement unwise at the time, and I cannot tell you how relieved I am to have you beside me. Rawlings is here with his family, and although he has apologised for his part in bringing Wickham to Pemberley, I am not comfortable having him so close.' His friend stretched out his booted legs towards the flames. 'It was a tactical nightmare trying to keep three beautiful young ladies safe from importunate young gentlemen last night. Having you there will make things easier – it was madness to come without a chaperone for Mary.'

'Is there not a mature matron somewhere that we know of who we could ask to join us?'

'Unfortunately my aunts are far too ancient to be of any practical use. Mrs Darcy or Mrs Bingley would have been ideal, but as they are both increasing they could not come.'

'Wait a minute, I have just thought of somebody who would be ideal. I have an older cousin. Her girls have both married well and her husband is involved with the East India Company and is seldom home.' He slammed his feet to the floor and jumped up. 'She lives in Romford and could be here by tomorrow morning if I can send your carriage to collect her.'

Adam looked sceptical. 'How can you be so sure she will come at a moment's notice? She could be away from home and then the carriage would have made a wasted journey.'

'Cousin Anthea prefers to travel in the summer. Although I do not correspond with her regularly, I occasionally call in to see her on my way back to barracks. The last time I spoke with her, a few months ago, she was bemoaning the fact that she never got to Town any more and missed the gaiety and excitement. I shall pen her a note immediately. Would you be kind enough to have the carriage ready to leave in a quarter of an hour?'

'Are we not to discuss this with either Kitty or Georgiana? I have a strong suspicion that neither of them will take kindly to us foisting a stranger on them.' Adam was also on his feet. 'However, as you are not to be here above a few nights it is essential I have the support of someone else reliable. Kitty so loves to dance and I do not like to deny her the opportunity. This means that there is no one on hand to keep Mary and Georgiana safe from predatory males.'

Jonathan shook his head in wonderment. 'How things have changed, old fellow – a year ago you would not have asked for help on such a matter. We are soldiers, can lead a regiment into battle without fear, but find ourselves quite at a loss in this milieu.'

They marched together through the house, he to find pen and ink, and his friend to send word to the stables. Was it Georgiana's role to speak to the housekeeper about preparing an apartment for Cousin Anthea? After all this was the Darcy house, but then Kitty was now a married woman and perhaps took precedence. He would leave this thorny problem to his friend; such matters were a minefield and not the concern of a rough soldier.

* * *

Georgiana was so happy she wanted to dance around the drawing room. She cared not why Jonathan had rushed to her side. All that mattered was that he was there and she would be able to appear on his arm tonight. 'Kitty, do you think there will be a waltz at the next ball we attend? Now that you are married you can do it. I hope that as I am engaged I too can join in.'

'I was disappointed they did not have one last night. I cannot wait to spin around the floor in the arms of my husband.' She clapped her hands to her mouth and scrambled to her feet. 'I have only had one lesson; I have never performed it in public.'

Immediately Mary put her journal aside. 'Would you like me to play for you both? I am sure that I know a suitable melody and you can go through the steps together. After all, we have been to private parties where young ladies have danced with each other when there have been insufficient gentlemen on hand.'

The pianoforte was at the far end of the drawing room, and there was ample space at that end of the chamber to put Mary's suggestion into practice. This dance was still considered fast, and those debutantes who attended the balls at Almack's were not allowed to do it until given permission by one of the dragons in charge.

Soon Mary was playing a lively tune and she and Kitty were attempting to perform the steps without the benefit of a gentleman to hold them upright. Twice she tripped over her skirt and the three of them were reduced to fits of giggles when the gentlemen rejoined them.

'Jonathan, you must dance with me. I fear I shall make an exhibition of myself if you lead me out for a waltz at the next ball without further practice.'

He sauntered towards them, but did not look especially eager. There was something wrong; his usual smile was absent. At once all desire to dance evaporated. 'What is wrong? Have you received bad news – do you have to return to Colchester?'

'Don't look so perturbed, my love; it's just that I know even less about this waltz than you do.' He turned to Adam. 'Can you demonstrate with Kitty? I am proficient in the reel, quadrille, country dances and the cotillion, but have never performed this new fashion.'

An enjoyable hour later Kitty insisted that Mary relinquish the piano stool and take her turn. At first she was reluctant, but then Adam charmed her into joining him on the makeshift dance floor. Within a short space of time she was whirling around as if she had been dancing the waltz forever.

'We have asked for a cold collation to be served in the small dining room, gentlemen. Shall you join us today or do you have something better to do?' Georgiana was not surprised they both agreed with alacrity. In a happy mood the party went to find their midday refreshments.

Once they were all seated Adam and Jonathan exchanged glances. Something was definitely up, for they looked quite shifty. 'Come along, what have you been up to? You must tell us at once, for you shall have no peace until you do so.'

'I have sent for my Cousin Anthea to join us here. The carriage should be in Romford within the hour, and might even return before nightfall bringing her to us. Mrs Darcy or Mrs Bingley should have been here to lend their support, my love, and we thought it might make things simpler if there was someone senior in your party to whom you could turn to for advice.'

'That is an excellent idea; we have discussed such a possibility ourselves but could come up with no one suitable. There really should be an older lady we can sit with if we are not dancing.'

'Tell us about your cousin, sir. Will she need to replenish her wardrobe? I am quite happy to forego the next few events until she is ready to accompany us, if that be the case.'

'Kitty, I am not an expert on these matters, but even to my untutored eye I would say she always looks elegant and fashionable. Her husband is generous with his allowance, and I believe she comes to London for her ensembles.'

'I take it that one of you also spoke to the housekeeper about preparing a chamber for her?'

'I did that, Georgiana, and the matter is already in hand,' Jonathan said.

'I believe there will be a dozen or more visitors this afternoon. I do hope you gentlemen will remain to support us?' Kitty asked, sending a stern look to her husband.

They agreed that they would be there, and the remainder of the mealtime passed with companionable chit-chat and there was barely time to run upstairs to tidy up before the first of the callers were due to arrive.

* * *

The minute hand was barely past the hour before the first arrivals appeared. Georgiana was sitting with Mary, and Kitty sat on her own with Adam standing guard behind her. However, once the guests began to pour in they were obliged to stand.

Two parlourmaids were in constant demand at the tea urn, which had been placed at the far end of the room, and two footmen circulated with almond biscuits and a variety of other beverages. Georgiana believed this must be the busiest house in Grosvenor Square this afternoon.

She was able to snatch a moment's conversation with Jonathan. 'The number of carriages calling here must be causing congestion outside. As no one stays above a quarter of an hour, the coachmen will be waiting and not move on to make room for the next arrival.'

'I had no idea morning calls were so frantic – I had imagined half a dozen elegant ladies sipping tea, not this crush.'

'Perhaps this is a common thing during the Season. No doubt our visitors move on to the next house. I suppose that we must return the compliment, but as I have little notion who most of these people are and no clue as to where they reside, I think that an impossible task.'

They were interrupted by a flurry of farewells as a Lady Something or Other departed with her three noisy daughters in tow. As expected several hopeful young gentlemen had been dragged along by their mamas, but none of them participated in the chatter; they hovered on the fringe looking uncomfortable. She rather thought that having Jonathan and Adam marching about the room might be the reason these visitors were so subdued.

Morning calls always finished at five o'clock, so the influx at a quarter to the hour should be the last. There were still a dozen or more visitors drinking tea and eating biscuits when she looked round to see Lady Rawlings, accompanied by her two daughters and her son, bustle into the drawing room.

Kitty greeted the family and led them to the tea urn. Jonathan and Adam had abandoned them half an hour since and there were no other gentlemen present.

'Miss Darcy, I bid you good afternoon. I have been traipsing from house to house since two o'clock this afternoon. I cannot tell you how tedious morning calls are for a gentleman.' Mr Rawlings bowed and accompanied his complaint with a charming smile. She could not take offence at his words, for she agreed with him.

'In which case there is no necessity to offer you refreshments – no doubt you are overflowing with tea and biscuits already.'

'I am indeed, but there has been a dearth of interesting conversation and that you can certainly supply.'

Somehow they had drifted apart from the crowd and were now standing alone. 'I fear I am quite out of any sort of conversation, let alone something interesting. Tell me, Mr Rawlings, were the other places as busy as here?'

'No, this has been the most popular.' He gestured towards the window. 'It is possible that the queue of carriages outside attracted those who had not intended to call themselves. My mother informed me that she could not recall the Darcy house being open to morning calls before. Naturally, everybody wishes to see inside the grandest house in the square.'

'Good gracious! I had not thought of that. We are not at home tomorrow or the next day, but I suppose I must resign myself to a similar experience the next time we open the doors to visitors.'

'I imagine that your ball will be the success of the Season, Miss Darcy. It is already the talk of the town; you must beware of gatecrashers for there are those that did not receive invitations who are determined to attend.'

The clock struck the quarter of an hour, cups and saucers were hastily put down, the last mouthful of biscuits swallowed, and there was a general exodus. Georgiana had no time to consider the implications of Mr Rawlings' comment but, as she was preparing for the evening, his words came back to her.

A shiver travelled down her spine. Had his remark been merely a pleasantry or was it a warning?

16

Mrs Anthea Bishop, Jonathan's cousin, arrived when Georgiana and the others were gathered in the drawing room after breakfast. He greeted her with affection and then introduced her to everybody. Mrs Bishop was of middle years, but her russet curls were still not tinged with grey and her figure trim and elegant.

'Thank you so much for inviting me to be your chaperone, Miss Darcy. I cannot tell you how delighted I am to be in London at this time. Mr Bishop is away until the autumn, my children have flown the nest, and I rattle around in my house on my own.'

'We are so pleased that you could come at such short notice, Mrs Bishop. You will be a very welcome addition to our party,' Georgiana said as she dipped in a curtsy.

Mary and Kitty greeted her with equal enthusiasm and soon she became Cousin Anthea to them all. She declared herself delighted with her accommodations and ready to escort Mary, Kitty and herself anywhere they wished to go. The gentlemen had already taken their leave, saying they had business to attend to in the city.

Scandal at Pemberley

'I should like to go to Gunter's to sample the ice cream,' Kitty announced. 'We could promenade along the street in our best bonnets and see what the world is doing this morning.'

'I have been there once or twice,' Georgiana replied, 'but would very much like to go again. If we feel the weather is too chilly to eat ice cream then we can have chocolate and cake instead.'

Mary agreed this was an excellent choice of excursion and they all retired to their chambers to put on their outdoor garments and boots.

Ellie held out a pelisse that matched Georgiana's gown. 'Are you going to wear this, miss, or your thick cloak?'

'That please, and the bonnet too. I know I would be warmer in my cloak, but I would not be so fashionable.' She smiled at her nonsense – when had she become so interested in her appearance?

She stepped away from the glass in order to view her image and was satisfied she looked her best. She tilted her head and her lips curved. 'This is a ridiculous hat, Ellie. Whatever possessed me to order it? The brim is far too deep and I shall not be able to see the person walking next to me.'

'You look ever so smart, Miss Darcy; everyone will be staring at you.'

Georgiana giggled. 'That is what I'm afraid of, but it is too late to do anything about it, for I cannot keep my friends waiting a moment longer. We are making calls this afternoon so will you have something suitable ready for me when I return?'

In fact she was the first to arrive in the hall and was adjusting her bonnet ribbons when there was a knock on the front door. A footman moved from his position in the shadows and walked briskly to open the door.

'Jonathan, I thought you were gone for the day.' She was so

delighted to see her beloved she quite forgot they were in full view of anyone descending the staircase.

'Sweetheart, I could not stay away a moment longer. I cannot think why I chose to go out with Adam when I have so little time to spend with you before I must return to Colchester.' He opened his arms and she flew into them.

His arms closed around her and she put her hands around his neck. His skin was cold, for he had gone hatless into the cool April morning. Then she forgot everything else as his mouth closed over hers in a hard, demanding kiss. She was lost to all sense of propriety; her senses swam and her blood fizzed around her body.

'Major Brownstone, that is quite enough. You might be engaged to Miss Darcy, but such behaviour is unacceptable even between a betrothed couple.'

Georgiana shot backwards almost losing her balance and would have moved away if he had not kept hold of her hand. She turned, her face scarlet, to see Cousin Anthea staring at them with disapproval.

Instead of being embarrassed by his cousin's reprimand, Jonathan laughed. 'You do not frighten me, my dear, but you are right to remind us to behave in public.'

'You are incorrigible, sir, and I think it would be a good idea if you returned to Colchester and remained there until the wedding.' Cousin Anthea's words were harsh, but her tone was light and her eyes twinkled.

'I beg your pardon, but I was so pleased to see Jonathan...'

'That was patently obvious, but I suggest that in future you both behave with more decorum if you are not to get yourselves a bad reputation.'

The sound of Kitty and Mary approaching ended the conversation not a moment too soon for Georgiana. Jonathan drew her to one side. 'I am coming with you, my love. I intend to be at your side every remaining minute that I am in Town.'

There was little point in suggesting that it would be a sad squash with five of them in the carriage. She knew him well enough to understand that he would not be dissuaded once he had made up his mind.

She sat with Mary and Kitty on one side and he sat with his cousin on the other, and every time she caught his eye he winked at her and she bubbled inside with happiness. Kitty squeezed her hand.

'I cannot believe how happy you look, dearest Georgiana. Now all we have to do is find Mary an eligible gentleman to fall in love with and then all the Bennet sisters will be settled.'

There was the spectre of Lydia between them, but neither of them mentioned it.

* * *

The time they spent at Gunter's was as enjoyable as it had been on her other visits and, apart from the fact that trying to spoon the delicious confection in her mouth whilst wearing a silly bonnet was almost impossible, Georgiana thought the excursion a resounding success.

Cousin Anthea fixed Jonathan with a basilisk stare. 'Well, at least you behaved yourself whilst we were out. I hope that you are not intending to accompany us on our morning calls as well?'

He was leaning in the corner with his long booted legs stretched sideways in the well of the carriage. He raised an eyebrow and shook his head sadly. 'I fear you are mistaken, my dear. I would not dream of allowing you to escort these diamonds of the first water to the houses of strangers without being there to offer my protection.'

Cousin Anthea snorted inelegantly. 'You're doing it too brown, sir; making morning calls is hardly a dangerous occupation.'

Georgiana was squashed into the corner, the one furthest away from him, and whilst still half-listening to the cousins bickering amiably she turned her attention to the streets outside. Her stomach lurched and she thought her ice cream about to return.

'Jonathan, I swear that I saw Lydia Wickham just now.' Her heart was thudding and her hands were clammy with dread.

'You must be mistaken, my love; they are safely at Longbourn and do not have the funds to travel, nor the means to convey themselves here.' Jonathan was now sitting straight, his expression serious.

Kitty tried to reassure her. 'The major is correct, dearest. Lydia has a common look about her; there must be a dozen or more young ladies who could be mistaken for her quite easily. Do you recall what she was wearing?'

Georgiana closed her eyes, trying to recapture the fleeting glimpse she had got of the girl she was convinced was her nemesis. 'She had on a cloak of dark blue and a bonnet with a pink lining.'

Kitty's smile vanished. 'I saw the very items you describe in Lydia's closet when she was at Pemberley. Oh dear! What shall we do now?'

'What is all this, Jonathan? There is something going on that I need to know about.'

He quickly gave his cousin the bare outlines of the matter and she pursed her lips and looked quite terrifying. As Georgiana stared at them she could see the family resemblance in both character and visage.

'I can see no reason to be worried, my dear Georgiana. Remember, you have both my cousin and Mr King to protect you, as well as myself. I can assure you that whatever mischief the Wickhams might be planning, they will not get near enough to you to cause you any upset.'

Somewhat reassured by this vehement comment, Georgiana unclenched her fists and managed a weak smile. 'What about Mr Rawlings? He will be at all the prestigious events, and for all his protestations I cannot bring myself to trust him.'

Jonathan stood up, making the coach rock alarmingly and stepped over the muddle of booted feet until he was repositioned opposite her. He reached across and took her trembling fingers within his own.

'I shall send word to Darcy and to Longbourn – we will discover how it is that Mr and Mrs Wickham have come to be in London when they are without funds.'

'Oh, you must not worry Lizzy, not in her delicate condition. Cousin Anthea is quite correct – I have both you and Adam here, and that will be sufficient to keep me safe.'

Kitty leaned forward so Georgiana could see her face; she was not reassured by what she saw. 'We are going to a musicale tonight. I think that should be perfectly safe, for at an informal event everyone will know each other and there is no chance that uninvited guests could find their way in.'

The words that Mr Rawlings had spoken to Georgiana the other night returned to her. She could not prevent a small shriek escaping. The other occupants swivelled to look at her in shock. 'I had forgotten to tell you all what Mr Rawlings said to me. He warned me to beware of gatecrashers.'

Jonathan's eyes narrowed and his lips thinned. 'Did he

indeed? I believe you might be right not to trust him, sweetheart; in fact I think it might be wise if you forego the pleasures of Town and return to Pemberley at once.'

'Nonsense, you are overreacting,' Cousin Anthea said firmly. 'No one is going to miss the jollity of their first Season. I know you cannot be here for more than a few days, Jonathan, but Mr King is more than up to the task of taking care of the young ladies in my charge.'

His fingers tensed around hers and Georgiana braced herself. No gentleman enjoyed being spoken to like that.

'Georgiana is my future wife and I shall decide what is best for her.' His tone was icy and the atmosphere in the carriage chilled. Mary and Kitty shrank back against the squabs and she withdrew her hands from his, not wishing to be part of this family squabble.

'I think that Georgiana is quite capable of making her own decisions. Do you wish to go home, my dear? Or do you trust those whose charge you are in to take care of you in the absence of your betrothed?'

'I have no wish to disagree with either of you, but I must own I do not enjoy being in London or attending balls and parties. I shall remain whilst Jonathan is here, but after that I shall go back.'

This announcement caused dismay. Both Kitty and Mary were horrified at her decision. 'Then Adam and I shall return as well,' Kitty said firmly.

'I agree with Georgiana; being squashed and ogled at is not something I enjoy. I too will return with you,' Mary said.

This was not what she had intended at all. 'No, I insist that you remain here. We can hardly cancel the invitations we have sent out to the ball in two weeks' time. Perhaps, on consideration, I shall reassess my previous comment. I might stay until the Darcy ball has taken place.'

Jonathan remained tight-lipped. 'I think this is best discussed in private, my love.'

The remainder of the journey was completed in an uncomfortable silence. Cousin Anthea had taken offence and Georgiana and her friends had no wish to make matters worse, so held their peace.

* * *

Lizzy snatched up the little brass bell that was placed on a side table within reach of her hand and rang it vigorously. Not for the first time she wished she was still nimble on her feet and able to run to find her husband and father. However, by the time she had regained her feet and waddled through the house, a servant could have fetched them both here.

A footman arrived in answer to her summons at the same time as Papa burst in through the doors that led to the library. She waved away the servant and held out the letter. 'I take it you have received a similar missive from Longbourn?'

'Indeed I have, my dear – it was so besmirched with tears that I could scarcely read it. This disaster is entirely my fault. I should never have let Mrs Bennet go home alone.' He collapsed onto an adjacent chair and dropped his head into his hands.

'Papa, have you sent word to Fitzwilliam? He must come at once to decide what action should be taken.'

His reply was indistinct as he did not look up, but she was sure he had said that he had not sent for her husband. She rang the bell again and this time the footman appeared immediately. 'Mr Darcy must be fetched; it is a matter of extreme urgency that he be found. If he is not within these walls then have men go around the estate until he is located.'

Her father continued to mutter and blame himself for his lack of forethought. She had no time for this, he must pull himself together so they could discuss this sensibly. 'Papa, sit up. We must talk. This is no more your fault than it is mine. How could either of us have known that Lydia would stoop so low as to steal from you? We have always known that Wickham is a flawed character; he left unpaid debts throughout the country when he ran away with my sister – Fitzwilliam was obliged to settle those as well as give him a substantial sum of money to marry her.'

'The day that man came into our lives was a disaster for the family. I'm sure that Lydia would not have behaved so reprehensibly without his encouragement. She has always been a silly girl, flighty and selfish, but never dishonest.' He delved into his jacket pocket and removed a handkerchief in order to wipe tears from his cheeks. 'She is lost to us now, Lizzy; she will never be welcome at Longbourn or anywhere else.'

They could not sit here wallowing in recriminations and misery. It would be bad for her and the babies. 'Papa, would you be so kind as to order coffee and refreshments to be brought here. It might be some time before Fitzwilliam can join us, and we need to have come up with some ideas before he does get here. Also I think that Jane and Bingley should be fetched from next door.'

Giving him something to do was the right move. He straightened his shoulders and began to look more like a man that she recognised, and not the shrivelled old gentleman he had temporarily become. Jane and Bingley arrived at the same time as the refreshments. When they had both read the letters they were equally distressed.

'Darcy and I must depart for London at once – God knows how many villains Wickham might have drawn into his scheme.' Bingley was not famous for his decision-making but today he appeared quite fierce.

'If we send a letter by express delivery that should arrive before either you or Darcy, should it not?' Jane said.

'I believe it would. They are delivered night or day. I well remember the one that came to Longbourn announcing that Lydia had run off with Wickham without benefit of clergy.' Papa was on his feet. 'I shall go at once and write a letter to King telling him what has transpired; he must be warned to be extra vigilant until we can apprehend the thieves.'

Lizzy exchanged a worried glance with her sister. 'He has taken Lydia's perfidy badly, Jane. I fear he will hand both of them over to the magistrate when they are found. I shall never be able to forgive our sister, but I would not wish for her to be thrown into jail.'

'I'm sure it will not come to that, although I should be sanguine about Wickham being incarcerated. Perhaps we can arrange for them to move permanently abroad, thus avoiding a scandal at Pemberley.'

The pounding of heavy boots alerted her to the arrival of Fitzwilliam. The doors crashed open and he erupted into the room, his face ashen and his hair in disarray. His sudden entry caused her to drop her coffee cup into her lap.

This accident was enough to restore his equilibrium. 'My darling, I feared you had had a mishap or gone into premature labour. Whatever the reason for my summons, it cannot be as bad as what I feared.'

'Don't stand there grinning at me like that, sir; help me to my feet so that I might return to our apartment and put on something dry. I shall explain why you were needed as we go.'

When he had heard the appalling story he was less upset than she was. 'I think you are refining too much on this, sweetheart. However much Wickham and Lydia stole it will not be sufficient to gain them entry to the *ton*. I think they will do their best to spread malicious rumours, but even if it reaches the ears of those who matter, they will dismiss it for what it is.'

He was acting as her lady's maid as they had no wish to have their conversation listened to by anyone, even staff as loyal as those working at Pemberley. Once she was freshly attired he put his arm around her and gently guided her back to join the others in the small drawing room.

More coffee had been fetched and the atmosphere in the chamber was a little less fraught. Her father had written his letter, and Jane and Bingley were reading it.

'Lizzy and I think that there is no need to overreact. A letter should suffice to warn King to pay extra vigilance when Georgiana is out and about.' He gestured to the missive. 'Might I be permitted to also read that, Mr Bennet?'

The paper was handed across and she watched him study it before he handed it to her. Now she understood the blank expressions upon her sister's and her husband's faces. The letter was so extreme in its vehemence, so exaggerated in the risk involved, that it could not possibly be sent.

Fitzwilliam nodded and folded the letter. 'Leave this to me, sir. I shall frank it myself and get it sent. If you would excuse me, I will deal with it immediately.' He was able to whisper to her as he pretended to fuss with her comforter, 'I shall pen another; he will never know.'

17

The musicale was as tedious as Georgiana had anticipated, even the appearance of Stefania Rovedino, a famous opera singer, could not save the evening. Mary was invited to perform but politely declined and the five of them left as early as was considered polite. Cousin Anthea had declined to accompany them, claiming she had the headache.

In the carriage on the way back, she sat with Mary and Kitty on either side and Adam and Jonathan were opposite. Despite the lateness of the hour the streets were busy; dozens of carriages rumbled in each direction over the cobbles and countless gentlemen, resplendent in top hats and cloaks, strode along the pavements.

'I sincerely hope we are not committed to attending another evening of such excruciating boredom,' Adam said from the darkness.

'I believe there are no more such events before our ball,' Georgiana told him. 'We are going to a private supper party tomorrow night – no, I should say tonight – and the following evening we go to the come-out ball for Lord Barnstable's daughter.'

'I can hardly wait, my love, but I fear that so much excitement is not good for a rough soldier.'

Georgiana was tempted to kick him but in her thin slippers she would come off worse. 'I cannot imagine why you gentlemen complain. We are the ones who are obliged to suffer on these grand occasions.'

The coach rocked as he sat upright and his knees pressed into hers. 'How is that possible? You ladies flit about in your beautiful gowns leaving us poor fellows to flounder in your wake.'

'You have no need to spend an age getting dressed – to have to make so many difficult decisions about what items to put on – you can appear in your uniform and Adam in his black, but Mary, Kitty and I cannot be seen in the same outfit twice.'

Kitty took up the refrain. 'Georgiana is quite correct. It would be easier if we were debutantes, then we could appear in white and one white gown looks very much like another.'

The carriage rocked to a halt outside their house and further conversation on this interesting topic was abandoned. Mary, who had fallen asleep, was picked up by Adam and carried in.

'My sister will not be happy about this, Georgiana; she does not like to be touched by anyone.'

'Your husband is being kind, Kitty. How can she object to that? Anyway, she probably will not remember how she got from the carriage to her bedchamber. I saw her consume two glasses of champagne and I believe the alcohol has sent her prematurely to sleep.'

Georgiana hurried ahead to open Mary's bedroom door for Adam. He placed his burden gently on the coverlet and with a friendly smile hurried after Kitty – no doubt to indulge in bedroom sport. A delicious warmth flooded through her at the thought of what that might entail. She could not wait until she was a wife like her dearest friend. She left Mary in the hands of her maid and stepped out into the flickering light of the sconces.

The passageway was deserted. Jonathan had his room on the far side of the building and Kitty and Adam had not waited to say goodnight. Her beloved had told her this evening that he could only spend two more nights away from his regiment and this meant she would be obliged to attend functions without his protection.

Her engagement was official; and she proudly wore the pretty diamond ring Jonathan had given her. Even without a ring on her finger no one could be in any doubt that she and Jonathan were betrothed. He had guarded her like a mother hen with a single chick and she had not been approached by either hopeful gentlemen or their mamas.

She wanted to return home when he left; she had no wish to remain in Town without him to escort her. In fact, strangely enough, Mary was the only member of their party who seemed eager to stay. Having originally insisted that she did not like gaiety of any sort, she had now quite changed her mind and was the liveliest of the three of them.

As Georgiana settled for the night, she tried to recall the names of the gentlemen who had paid Mary attention tonight. None of them were exceptional, although one did seem to have caught Mary's eye. What was his name? She frowned in the darkness, trying to bring his features to the forefront of her mind.

The young man had been above average height with mouse-brown hair and regular features – she could not recall his name however hard she tried – but she did remember he had eyes of a strange violet colour and a charming smile. He had escorted Mary into supper and she had enjoyed his attention.

She must ask Kitty if he was eligible before Mary's affections were engaged. The fact that Fitzwilliam had made Mary a substantial heiress, as well as her being an attractive young lady, had elevated her to the status of being one of the most sought-after young ladies of the year. How much had changed in the last six months and all of it for the better.

* * *

The informal supper party turned out to be a far grander occasion than any of them had anticipated. There were more than a hundred guests and provision had been made for those who wished to play cards, for those who wished to converse in a quiet environment, but also for those who wished to dance. A trio of elderly aunts were to take turns at the piano throughout the evening.

The only drawback had been the sad squash in the carriage. Mary had been obliged to sit on Adam's lap in order to accommodate Cousin Anthea.

'Well, my dears, this is all most satisfactory,' Cousin Anthea said as she looked around the gathering. 'Sufficient people to make the evening interesting, but not so many as to make it a crush.'

'Mary, Mr Colby is approaching. Do you wish to dance with him or shall I scare him off?'

'I would prefer to stay with you all for the moment, Mr King, so I would be most grateful if you could prevent him from asking me. If I refuse then I shall be unable to dance later if I change my mind.'

Adam intercepted the young man and spoke quietly to him. Mr Colby nodded and headed off towards the card room.

'What did you say to him? I do hope he didn't take offence,' Mary said when Adam returned.

'I told him you intended to play cards but would be delighted to dance after supper. So I suppose we had better find a table and play a hand or two.'

The card room was filling up and they had difficulty finding a table with six empty chairs, but between them Adam and Jonathan succeeded. Once they were all seated, Cousin Anthea took charge. 'Shall we play a hand or two of Loo? I assume that all of you know the rules and it is a game that can accommodate any number of players.'

After an enjoyable half an hour Georgiana put down her cards. 'I think it is silly for us to be playing cards here when we could do so perfectly well at home. I wish to dance. I am sure that I overheard someone saying there was to be a waltz or two played tonight and I have yet to perform this in public.'

Kitty was on her feet immediately. 'We must go at once. I too long to waltz with my husband.'

'Mary, my dear, you must not accept an invitation to waltz – in my opinion it is a fast dance and best left to young ladies who are already spoken for,' Cousin Anthea said.

'I believe that might be the case, ma'am, at Almack's and if one was a debutante. But I have been out these past two years and believe it will be acceptable for me to waltz if I am invited.' Mary's eyes were sparkling and she looked quite enchanting.

'In which case, I shall say no more. However, I would suggest that you don't dance with anyone you have not been formally introduced to. I'm sure that you have no wish to appear a flighty miss.'

Mary dipped in a curtsy but did not reply. As they made

their way towards the sound of the piano being played with more verve than skill, Georgiana took Jonathan's arm.

'No doubt Mary will be waiting for an invitation from Mr Colby. He seems a pleasant enough young man but I wish we knew more about him.'

'Adam and I can make enquiries tomorrow. Until then we will keep a sharp eye on them and see that nothing untoward takes place.'

When they reached the room set aside for dancing there was an eager buzz of anticipation amongst those waiting there. At the first notes of a waltz, a ripple of excitement flooded through her. Jonathan took her hand and led her onto the floor.

The experience was magical. She felt like a princess in a fairy tale as she was whisked around the floor in the arms of the man she loved. She scarcely had time to take notice of who else was dancing, but when the waltz came to an end she glanced around.

'Look, Mary did dance with Mr Colby.' As she watched, the young man bowed and led his partner back to Cousin Anthea. Only then did Georgiana become aware that the beady eyes of several tabbies appeared to be fixed on Mary.

'Do you see that, Jonathan? I fear Mary might have become the focus of disapproval from the matrons sitting over there.'

'My cousin appears to have drawn the same conclusion. She has sent Mr Colby packing and is on her feet. I believe we are beating a retreat before insurmountable opposition.'

Despite the gravity of the situation she could not stop a bubble of mirth escaping. 'We cannot leave until we have Kitty and Adam. They are not on the dance floor – surely they participated? Kitty was so eager to waltz.'

Cousin Anthea greeted them with a tight smile. 'This is an unmitigated disaster. I knew Mary should not waltz in public, but she would go her own way and now her reputation is in tatters.'

'That's coming it a bit strong, Cousin. This is an informal party; she was supervised at all times. How can this have damaged her good name?'

They were now heading for the stairs and Kitty and Adam were waiting for them, their expressions grave. Throughout this retreat Mary had been silent. She did not protest at being removed from the gaiety; indeed, a small smile played about her lips as if she knew something they did not.

Once they were safely in their carriage, the reason for the hurried exit became clear. 'It would seem that Colby is not what he appears. He has a reputation for playing fast and loose with a young lady's affections.'

'How dreadful! But hopefully the damage has been minimal. Mary has only danced with him twice and has never been alone in his company.' Georgiana put her hand on Mary's but she moved hers away as if resenting her touch.

As soon as they were home Mary retired, leaving the five of them to discuss the disaster. Cousin Anthea said what they were all thinking. 'Mary spent far too much time with Mr Colby at the musicale and this was also noted by those who were there. She seems in a fair way to falling under his spell.'

'I have discovered Colby is the son of a wealthy landowner and although not exactly rich, he has more than enough blunt not to be considered a fortune hunter,' Adam said.

'I'm not sure if that is worse than being a philanderer,' Cousin Anthea said gloomily. 'We must endeavour to keep Mary safe from him. In future she must dance only with gentlemen that have been vetted by us.' She put down her teacup and saucer. 'I shall retire. I apologise for my failure tonight – I should have been more vigilant.'

Kitty and Adam soon followed Cousin Anthea, leaving her and Jonathan alone. He yawned and then apologised. 'I find all this gallivanting damnably tiring, sweetheart. I would much rather be outside in the fresh air than cooped up with overdressed, over-perfumed strangers.'

'I agree with you; I am not enjoying my time in Town. Does that make me an unnatural young lady? Are we not supposed to enjoy every minute of our Season?'

'In which case, you will not be sad to return to Pemberley after the ball?'

'I should like to go back immediately; I don't like to be away whilst Lizzy and Jane are in an interesting condition.'

He moved slowly towards her and her heart skipped a beat. She closed the gap and he encircled her with his arms, drawing her closer until her cheek rested against the rough fabric of his uniform. She sighed, relaxing into his embrace, knowing this was where she was meant to be.

They stood like this for a few moments and then he kissed the top of her head. 'We must retire. We are keeping the servants up unnecessarily. I am counting the days until you become my wife. Even though you have said you wish to remain with your brother until I am discharged, I'm beginning to think that you would actually enjoy following the drum.'

'I had been intending to speak to you on this subject, my love, for I have come to the same conclusion. If you consider it safe for me to be with you abroad, then I shall come. Of course, I would not remain once I was increasing.'

His arms tightened and she looked up expectantly. This kiss was long and lingering, his mouth demanding against hers and the pleasure and thrill of it made her go weak at the knees. With obvious reluctance he raised his head and brushed a thumb across her swollen lips.

'Goodnight, darling, we will talk of this again in the morning.'

* * *

Georgiana was rather dreading going down for breakfast, as she fully expected there to be some sort of scene from Mary when she was told she could no longer be associated with Mr Colby. In fact the girl accepted the news with a shrug.

'I scarcely know him; he is a very attractive gentleman and an excellent dancer. However, I was not developing a *tendre* for him, if that is what you all feared.'

Cousin Anthea, who was leading the discussion, nodded her approval. 'I'm delighted to hear you say so, my dear. If you behave with modesty and decorum for the next few days I am sure the incident will soon be forgotten.'

'I wish to purchase fresh ribbons for my best bonnet, Georgiana. Would you and Kitty care to come with me?' Mary looked from one to the other hopefully.

'I intend to spend the morning lazing about indoors,' Kitty said, 'but will rouse myself if you really need me to accompany you.'

'Jonathan and I intend to ride in the park, so I'm afraid I cannot come,' Georgiana added.

Mary turned to Cousin Anthea. 'Do I have your permission to go by myself?'

'I have no objection, my dear, as long as you take a footman and your maid. The walk is no more than half a mile and Bond Street is a perfectly acceptable place for a young lady to promenade without an escort.'

The breakfast party split up – Georgiana needed to go upstairs to change into her riding habit, Kitty decided to play billiards with Adam, and Mary went to get ready to go out. Georgiana followed Kitty and Adam, Jonathan close behind.

'Kitty, I wish to speak to you. I have some serious concerns about Mary. From what you have told me about your sister I had thought her a quiet, studious young lady and yet here she is gadding about Town, and fluttering her eyelashes at Mr Colby.'

'Mary has always been in the background. Lizzy and Jane were papa's favourites; Lydia and I were mama's. She has always been considered the plainest of the Bennet sisters. Indeed, I often heard my mother say that she expected Mary to remain a spinster and to spend her days at Longbourn looking after her and Papa.'

'Small wonder the poor girl is kicking up her heels,' Jonathan said. 'We must just ensure she is kept safe from any further predatory young men. She is an innocent and could easily be hoodwinked by an unscrupulous gentleman.'

'I am at a loss to understand why Mr Colby made his attentions so plain – what could he hope to gain? He might have a slightly unsavoury reputation, but I am sure he is not a hardened rake.' Georgiana looked at Kitty for an answer.

'I have no idea, dearest...'

'I think I might have the answer, Georgiana. It could have been a wager. Young bucks will gamble on anything,' Jonathan said.

Adam nodded in agreement. 'I think you have the nub of it, my friend. Colby was with a group of young men and could well have been challenged to persuade a debutante to waltz with him.'

'Do you think so? That is a relief – perhaps you and Jonathan could verify that this afternoon whilst we are making morning calls?' Georgiana hurried off to change, happy with the outcome of the conversation.

18

There had been no social engagement that night and Georgiana was pleased to spend the evening with her family and friends in the comfort of her own home. Tomorrow night was the Barnstable ball and they were all agreed they would need a quiet night before that event.

'We asked about Colby,' Jonathan said, as they were gathering around the tea urn. 'It is as we suspected, there is a wager entered in the book at White's that he would be the first to dance a waltz with a debutante.'

Mary had retired early with a megrim and so was not there to hear this distressing news.

'If I see him again I can promise you that he will not enjoy the encounter,' Adam said grimly.

'I think it would be best to let the matter drop, dearest, for Mary's sake. I expect he and his cronies will be at the ball tomorrow night so we must all be vigilant on her behalf.' Kitty looked to Cousin Anthea, who nodded vigorously.

'I can assure you that I will not let any gentleman near her unless they have been previously introduced to us by a reputable person.' She paused as if not sure whether her next remark might be unwelcome. 'I am not sure if either you or Georgiana were aware that Mary came back without the ribbons she said she needed so urgently. I questioned her maid and the footman, and they said that she went instead to Hatchards and that they were unable to keep her in sight for the entire time she was there.'

'Do you think she had an assignation of some sort? Are they quite sure that Colby was not there?' Kitty asked anxiously.

'As far as I can ascertain there were no gentlemen amongst the shelves that Mary visited. However, she could have spoken to any number of young ladies as the place was packed with them.'

Georgiana's cup rattled on its saucer. 'Jonathan, do you think she might have met up with Lydia?'

Adam got to his feet, his expression serious. 'I think that is highly unlikely unless someone in this establishment is in league with the Wickhams.'

'The staff here are loyal; we have employed nobody new this age. We are refining too much on this. I'm sure that if Mary were here she would explain her change of mind.'

Jonathan was now also standing. 'Cousin Anthea, did Mary bring back any books?'

'Not as far as I am aware, but then I did not ask about books, only about ribbons. I fear this mystery must remain until we can question Mary tomorrow morning. Hopefully her headache will have gone by then and she will be able to join us for breakfast.'

The party broke up and Georgiana had no opportunity to linger and spend time alone with her beloved. Tomorrow would be his last night in London, and heaven knows when they would be together again.

***

A few hours later Jonathan was roused by a thunderous knocking on the front door. As all the family rooms faced the rear of the building, it was unlikely anyone else would be disturbed by the racket. He scrambled out of bed and snatched up his dressing robe, wishing he had had the foresight to put on his nightgown before retiring.

There was sufficient light filtering in through the shutters to tell him that dawn had already broken. There was no necessity for him to light a candle; he would be able to find his way downstairs without one. The banging continued – surely one of the servants must be aware there was somebody demanding to be let in?

He took the stairs three at a time, regretting with every stride that he had neglected to put on his boots before leaving his bedroom. As he reached the front door he heard the sound of others approaching from below stairs. Should he wait or open the door himself?

Devil take it! If he didn't stop this noise, the entire street would be awake. He pushed back the bolts, turned the key and flung the door open.

A dishevelled, mud-spattered man handed him a letter. 'Express delivery from Derbyshire, sir. Do you wish me to wait for a reply?'

As Jonathan was not dressed he had no coins in his pocket with which to reward the exhausted man.

'Allow me, major, I have the necessary with me.' Robinson was almost correctly dressed; only a slight bulge beneath his immaculate black coat indicated he still had his nightshirt on beneath it.

'I shall leave you to deal with it, thank you.' Jonathan

retreated, the letter in his hand. There was a tightness in his chest as he turned it over and saw it was addressed to Adam. This could only be bad news – no one sent good news by express delivery.

He sent up a heartfelt prayer to God that both Mrs Darcy and Mrs Bingley were well. There was nothing for it – he must wake Adam and give him the letter immediately. If Darcy had gone to the trouble and expense of sending the letter by express then the contents must be urgent indeed.

The butler bolted the door and was on his way across the hall to join him. 'Mr King's bedchamber is the third door on the right.'

Jonathan nodded his thanks and bounded up the stairs to deliver the letter. He knocked softly and a few moments later footsteps approached the door.

'Adam, a letter from Derbyshire has just arrived,' he said softly, not wishing to worry Kitty who would still be in bed.

The door opened a fraction. 'I will be there in a moment. I must get dressed. Meet me in the study in five minutes.'

Jonathan didn't argue; this would give him time to put some clothes on as well. Better that he and Adam discovered what was within the missive before Georgiana, Kitty or Mary were involved. He was on his way within the allotted time, decently, but not correctly attired. There had been no time to find a waistcoat or tie his neckcloth, but at least he now had boots and breeches on.

The tall clock struck four – another two hours before the house would be alive with servants. He headed for the study and was astonished to find the shutters had been drawn back and a tray of coffee stood steaming gently on the desk. Robinson was a marvel; the man appeared to anticipate their every wish.

He poured two cups of the dark, aromatic brew and was

sipping his when Adam arrived. 'The letter is on the desk. I pray it is not bad news about either of the ladies.'

His friend broke the seal and opened the paper. There was a silence and then Adam laughed. 'Thank God for that – everyone is well at Pemberley. Darcy is just confirming what we already know: that the Wickhams are in London and we should take extra care of Georgiana. He is unaware that you are with us, but I can tell you, my friend, I am glad that you are here.'

'Do not leave me dangling, old fellow, what else does he say?'

'It would appear the two of them removed all the valuables from Longbourn and ran away in the Bennet carriage. At least that explains how they can afford to be here; they will have sold their ill-gotten gains to raise the necessary funds.'

'I must go to Horse Guards this morning and ask for extra furlough. I cannot return to Colchester if there is the slightest danger to Georgiana.'

'I shall remain here until Kitty is ready to return – we had no wedding trip and this will be her only opportunity to attend parties and so on until after the Pemberley babies are born. I have your cousin here to chaperone Mary, so why don't you ask Georgiana if she wishes to return immediately?'

'We have already discussed this possibility; she told me she wishes to leave London when I do. We will attend the ball tonight and then I shall escort her home the next day.'

'You can only do that if you are granted extra leave, my friend, and I think that unlikely. She wouldn't want you to get yourself cashiered over this. Travelling in the Darcy carriage with two outriders and two on the box, Georgiana will be quite safe.'

'I have already taken more time from my duties than I should; there is a war with France coming soon and I shall be needed to lead my men. I will take your advice and return to Colchester as planned. I sincerely hope I am in the country in September so our nuptials can go ahead.'

There was a soft tap on the door and the butler stepped in. 'Do you require anything else, gentlemen?'

'No, we are returning to our beds and you must do the same. There is no need for any of us to be up at this ungodly hour.' Jonathan yawned loudly and Adam laughed, and Robinson almost smiled.

'It is half an hour after four. The sun will be up soon, hardly seems worthwhile retiring for an hour or two. Shall we go for a gallop around the park instead?'

'An excellent idea – we have been cooped up indoors for too long.' Jonathan nodded at the butler. 'There is no need to rouse the grooms, we shall take care of our own horses.'

'Very well, sir, I shall ensure that breakfast is ready for your return. I shall also unbolt the side door before I return to my chamber.'

* * *

After an invigorating two hours thundering around the deserted park, Jonathan returned to Grosvenor Square feeling happier and healthier than he had these past few days. The streets were now alive with folk going about their early morning business – although these were servants and tradespeople – the gentry would still be snug in their beds at this hour.

'I shall join you in the breakfast parlour in an hour, Adam; hopefully Georgiana will be down by then. I sincerely hope the girls do not have plans to go out and about today. I do not feel that Wickham presents a genuine danger, but I have no wish for there to be any unpleasantness.'

'Kitty did not mention anything, but we will persuade them to stay here until we go out tonight. Do you still intend to visit Horse Guards?'

'I might as well as I am in Town. Perhaps somebody there will know what is going on in France.'

* * *

Georgiana was just about to leave her bedchamber and go down to break her fast when there was a tap on her sitting room door. Ellie looked at her enquiringly.

'You wish me to answer that, Miss Darcy?'

'There is no need. I am going out myself so will see who it is.' She stepped out of her bedchamber and saw Jonathan poised to knock again outside her sitting room.

'Good morning, I did not expect a visit at this time of the day.'

His smile made her toes curl. 'I have been up since the crack of dawn – can we go back into your sitting room so we can talk privately?'

Intrigued, but not especially concerned as he did not look at all worried, she smiled her acquiescence and gestured that he enter. She followed him and before she could protest he had swept her up into his arms and kissed her soundly.

She was breathless when he returned her to her feet. 'You must not do that, Jonathan. We will give Ellie palpitations.'

'I don't give a damn what your maid says – however, I shall refrain from kissing you if that is what you want.'

'What I want, my love, is for you to refrain from swearing. Now, what has brought you here?'

When he had explained and asked her opinion on the matter she was ready with her answer. 'If Kitty and Mary have no objection, I shall be delighted to go back home, for I much prefer to be in the country than in Town.' She shook her head sadly. 'I am deeply shocked that Lydia has become a common thief. It must be so distressing for her parents. Lizzy and Jane will be in need of my support at this difficult time.'

'You must remember, sweetheart, she was fifteen years old when she married, scarcely a woman grown. Her life has not been easy since Wickham was discharged with dishonour from the military and has yet to find himself an honourable profession.'

'I'm quite certain that both Lizzy and Jane have been supporting their sister these past months but even they might well abandon her entirely after this. You are right, she has been led astray by the true villain. We should be offering her sympathy and not condemnation.'

He brushed her cheek with his fingers. 'The more I know you, the more I love you; I must be the luckiest man in Christendom to have gained your heart. I was talking to Adam earlier, and the news is grim from the continent. This upstart Napoleon Bonaparte will crown himself emperor and will be turning his attentions to Britain very soon.'

'I have no wish to talk about this. The very thought of you being involved in such things makes me heartsick. I wish you were not a soldier but a gentleman of leisure like Adam.'

'Darling girl, I am the third son of a baron, have no inheritance and only my military stipend and prize money to my name. I cannot resign my commission. Every experienced officer will be required when the war with France recommences.'

'I shall say no more on the subject, but I wish we were to be wed immediately, before you leave to fight.' No sooner had she said this than she decided this would be her goal. 'If Fitzwilliam gives his permission, would you be prepared to marry me immediately? By special licence? I shall not come with you – I know that would be too dangerous – but at least we will have become man and wife before you go. Once the fighting starts, you will not get leave of absence, possibly for years, and I could not bear to wait that long to become your wife.'

Instead of being shocked by her request he nodded. 'I have thought the same myself. I shall apply for a special licence when I'm out this morning and ask for an extra week of leave so that we can be married as soon as we get to Pemberley.'

'It will mean being married with only half of our families in attendance – not the ceremony I had envisaged – but in the circumstances it is the one I want.'

'We shall be spending the evening together at the ball, and I shall dance every dance with you and set the tabbies gossiping. If we let it be known we are to be married immediately then I am sure your reputation will remain intact.'

'I am so excited I could burst. We must go downstairs and tell the others what we have decided. I shall be sad not to have Kitty and Mary at our wedding, but I would not dream of driving them away from Town when they are having such fun.'

Happily, everyone was in the breakfast parlour and once she and Jonathan had filled their plates, the footmen were dismissed. The conversation was of the shocking news about the Wickhams, but Georgiana had something even more sensational to tell them.

'We have something we wish to say; I do hope you will not be too appalled.'

Once the news had been imparted, there was a stunned silence. Adam shook his head and shrugged, as if dismissing responsibility for the whole thing. Cousin Anthea was the first to speak.

'I am surprised by your announcement, but not dismayed. I think you have the right of it, my dear. Either you must get married immediately or endure a protracted and worrying engagement. However, do you think that Mr Darcy will agree?'

Kitty recovered her voice and chimed in. 'We must all return with you. I cannot bear to miss your wedding.'

'You cannot do that, dearest. The Darcy ball is to be held in less than a sennight and it can hardly go ahead without someone to present.' Georgiana turned to Mary. 'It shall be your night. I shall be delighted to hand the honour to you.'

Mary dropped her cutlery with a clatter. 'If we are to miss your wedding then we must spend the day together. I am sure there must be items you will need that you have not purchased as yet. Kitty, you must be our guide in this.'

'There will be no time to make you bride clothes, but you already have a closet full of new gowns, so I'm sure that is no obstacle,' Kitty said.

Jonathan banged the table, bringing the conversation to an immediate halt. 'Ladies, neither Adam nor I wish to hear so frivolous a conversation whilst eating our breakfast. Kindly get on with your meal and let us do the same.' He glared at them in mock ferocity and Mary giggled.

'I beg your pardon, Major Brownstone, Kitty and I will take Georgiana to Bond Street after breakfast and you will hear no more on the subject of feminine fripperies.'

When they had finished it was agreed they would not meet the gentlemen again until dinner, which was to be served early tonight so they could leave in plenty of time for the ball. Although the distance to this grand event was short there would be such a crush of carriages that it would take some time to reach their destination.

Less than an hour later, the three of them were ready to

depart. Georgiana had almost forgotten about the letter from Fitzwilliam that had been the catalyst for persuading her and Jonathan to marry. As the weather was clement they were to walk the short distance to the emporiums, but they had a ridiculously large escort of three personal maids, two footmen and an unknown gentleman in a smart brown topcoat.

'Surely, Kitty, we do not require quite so many to accompany us? And who is the gentleman bringing up the rear of our party?'

Her friend smiled knowingly. 'The maids and the footmen are coming to carry our purchases. Brownlow – the man of business – is there to sign the chits. No doubt we shall spend a prodigious amount of money today.'

19

When they arrived at Bond Street Georgiana was surprised to find the pavements already crowded with shoppers. 'Good heavens! Why are there so many people here today?'

'I have no notion, but the haberdashers we wish to visit is directly ahead. We can go in there and then send Brownlow to discover what all the fuss is about.'

One of their footmen held open the door to the emporium and Georgiana led the charge inside. She had not expected to see so many customers, but there was barely room to move.

She was buffeted by an elderly matron in a startling turban, wielding a walking stick. 'I do beg your pardon, madam, I hope I did not step on your toes,' Georgiana said hastily, not liking the beady look she was being given.

Immediately the matron's face relaxed and she half-smiled. 'Prettily said, my dear. It is a sad crush today, and no mistake. Believe me, if I had known that the prince was to parade down Bond Street, I should have remained at home until tomorrow.'

That explained the throng of people outside. 'I had no idea

the future king visited such a place as Bond Street. Is he expected soon, do you know?'

'According to my maid, the prince should be here very soon. You and your friends would be better served by remaining safely in this place, and not venturing outside again until he has gone.'

'I think you might be right, ma'am. I shall pass this information on to my companions.' Georgiana could see Kitty and her maid examining a stand of ribbons, but of Mary there was no sign. She was scanning the bobbing bonnets in the shop but then glanced out of the window and saw Mary and her maid outside. What were they doing out there? She waved and she was almost sure that Mary saw her, but then they moved off and were out of sight.

'Ellie, tell Mrs King that Miss Bennet has gone off somewhere on her own and that I am going after her.' Without waiting to see if the girl did as she was bid, Georgiana hurried to the exit. She looked for one of the footmen so he could accompany her, but they were not outside the door. They must be close by, and in this press of people she should be safe enough.

There were carriages of all descriptions queueing in the street. She overheard a pedestrian say that the prince had gone past and this had caused the jam of vehicles. There was no sign of either of the footmen – where on earth could the wretched men have gone? Then she saw the two of them standing a goodly distance away gawping after the future monarch.

Botheration! She stood on tiptoes and could just see the top of Mary's head. If she waited for the footmen to return she would lose her altogether. She had no option but to hurry after the girls without an escort and just pray that in the crowd, even if either of the Wickhams were here, they could not possibly pick her out.

By keeping close to the shopfronts she was able to make steady progress and was certain she was gaining on her quarry. Then to her horror a tall, fair-haired gentleman appeared from a doorway and took Mary's arm. She recognised him, even from this distance, as Mr Colby. Mary had made an assignation – how could she be so foolhardy? What if someone recognised her?

As she watched the two of them disappeared and she increased her pace. They must have turned into Grafton Street and she knew that this led through Dover Street and into Albemarle Street where many gentlemen had their lodgings.

She saw them as soon as she turned the corner – thank goodness the maid was within arm's reach, and even though the two of them were talking earnestly, nothing had yet occurred that could be detrimental to a young lady's reputation. Mary was becoming agitated – something was not right.

Georgiana was about to call out when the door of the carriage she was hurrying past opened, and before she could call out, she was dragged into it. An evil-smelling bag was dropped over her head and shoulders, making it impossible for her to struggle or scream for help.

* * *

Lizzy thought Pemberley seemed empty now that her father had left for Longbourn. He had said that he could travel by public coach, but Fitzwilliam had insisted he take one of the Darcy carriages. After all he no longer had the one that he had been given when Jane and she had married last year.

'I believe our children are having a boxing match, my love. I shall be black and blue inside before they make their appearance in this world.'

He looked up from the journal he was perusing. 'You are

more than two thirds of the way through your pregnancy, sweetheart. Before you know it the babies will be here and then you will be wishing them back inside again.'

Lizzy snatched up a cushion and threw it at her husband's head – her aim was poor, and it tore through the middle of his newspaper. His look of incredulity made her forget her momentary irritation at his callous disregard for her feelings.

'What the devil are you about? I almost suffered from an apoplexy. Why are you throwing things at me?' He tossed the mangled paper to one side and got to his feet.

'I beg your pardon, Fitzwilliam, I don't know what came over me. If you had the slightest understanding of what I have to endure, then perhaps you would not have made such a fatuous remark.'

He dropped to his haunches beside her and took her hands in his, gently raising them to his lips and then kissing each knuckle in turn. 'It is I who must apologise, darling. I spoke without thought. Whilst I am up, is there anything you would like me to fetch for you?'

'Would you be kind enough to see if there has been any mail delivered? There could be a reply from London or possibly one of the girls might have written to me. I am feeling rather flat today...'

His snort of laughter made her realise how silly her comment must have sounded and she reached for a second missile to throw at him. He raised his hands in surrender. '*Mea culpa!* Forgive me, I should not laugh...'

'Indeed you should not, Mr Darcy. I believe my sense of humour disappeared at the same time as my toes.'

Still chuckling he wandered off to see what, if anything, had been delivered. She smiled at her silliness. Jane had remained the same serene and sunny-natured person she had always been; it was only she who had turned into a termagant since she had been increasing.

Fitzwilliam was taking an unconscionable time fetching the letters. Slowly she pushed herself upright and was in the process of swinging her feet to the floor when he appeared. She scarcely recognised the man standing in the doorway with an open letter in his hand. His face was grey and pinched. It was as if he had aged ten years.

'What is it? Tell me at once what the letter says.'

He was incapable of speech and walked swiftly across to her, tossed the missive in her lap, then collapsed on the end of the daybed and dropped his head into his hands.

Darcy,

By the time you receive this letter, your precious sister will be in my hands. Miss Bennet and Colby have made her abduction possible. Rawlings is going to marry Georgiana and there is nothing you can do about it.

With Rawlings' seed in her belly she will have no choice – Major Brownstone will be glad to be shot of her.

I am not doing this for monetary gain but for revenge. I shall have destroyed the life of Georgiana Darcy; she will be as miserable as I in her marriage, and you can do nothing about it. It is too late for you to intervene – the damage is done.

You will not find me. I leave for the continent tomorrow. However, you may inform your wife that if she wishes to collect her snivelling sister, then she is free to do so as I shall not be taking her with me.

A wave of dizziness made Lizzy's head swim. Small wonder

Fitzwilliam was incapable of speech. She read the letter a second time and her nausea receded. She clutched Fitzwilliam's arm. 'My love, this is not as bad as it might appear. Wickham has written you a letter, but it does not mean the contents are true.'

He stirred beside her and slowly raised his head. His colour began to return and he looked more like the man she knew and loved. 'Go on, Lizzy, I am listening.'

'That monster could write anything he wished – we have no way of verifying the contents. You and Charles must go at once to London. I am sure you will find Georgiana safe and well in Grosvenor Square. I shall send word immediately to Sir Matthew – he must come here and speak to me about his son. The boy has always seemed rather wild, but I cannot credit he would become involved in something so base.'

'God's teeth! Thank God I have you at my side to speak common sense. My wits were wandering; now I see things more clearly. Bingley and I will certainly go to London, and then with King's help we will track down that bastard Wickham and deal with him once and for all.'

He surged to his feet and without a second glance strode off shouting for attention. She heard him greeting Charles and then Jane was at her side. Lizzy handed her the letter but explained that she did not think it true. 'Adam will have had Fitzwilliam's letter warning him that Wickham and Lydia were in London – he would not have allowed Georgiana out without proper protection.'

Jane nodded. 'I agree, dearest Lizzy. Have you sent for Sir Matthew to ask him what he thinks of this?'

'I intend to do so now. Shall we bid our husbands a safe journey?'

Within less than a quarter of an hour Fitzwilliam and

Charles were ready to depart. They were not taking a valet with them, and had only a valise to carry.

'Take care, my love, and do not do anything you might regret later.'

'I shall do what is necessary, my love, and live with the consequences. I will send word by express as soon as I arrive – we must both pray your interpretation of this situation is the correct one. If anything has happened to Georgiana...'

Lizzy could no longer embrace her husband as she had used to do, as the bulk of her pregnancy intruded. She quickly turned sideways and reached out to touch his cheek. Immediately he covered her hand with his and tenderly kissed the palm. Then he drew her close and kissed her.

'Promise me, my love, you will take care.'

His eyes were hard, his expression uncompromising. 'I will be careful, Lizzy, and I shall return with my sister safe and well.' Without a further word being spoken he was gone with only the sound of the door closing to remind her of his departure.

Sir Matthew and Lady Rawlings arrived two hours later. One look at their demeanour was enough to make her heart sink. 'Thank you for coming so promptly. I believe that you might know why I have asked you here.'

Sir Matthew was having difficulty controlling his emotions; Lady Rawlings delved into her reticule and produced a handkerchief to dab her eyes. 'We do indeed, Mrs Darcy, and expected to find Mr Darcy here as well. This morning we had a letter from our son saying that he and Miss Darcy are to be married today. We knew this would be without your consent. The wretched boy must have obtained a special licence and eloped with her.'

Lizzy closed her eyes and it was as if a large boulder had settled on her chest. She had given her husband false hope –

their beloved Georgiana had indeed been abducted and it was already too late to save her from the most dreadful fate.

* * *

Jonathan left Horse Guards satisfied with the outcome of his visit. He had been given two weeks' leave in order to get married and only then would have to return to his regiment. After that he would have no further opportunity to go home until Bonaparte had been defeated – God knows how many years that might be.

However, he was beginning to have second thoughts about this hurried marriage. If he were to be killed, or even worse be maimed for life, then would this be fair to Georgiana? Surely it would be better, the gentlemanly thing to do, to break the engagement and leave her free to find happiness elsewhere?

The thought of her in the arms of another man was like a dagger in his heart. But he loved her too much to drag her into the world of a professional soldier, so would do the right thing. He would escort her to Pemberley and leave her in the care of her brother and then sever the relationship.

He swallowed the lump in his throat and decided to go to his club and drown his sorrows. In his distress, he failed to watch his way and collided with a stout gentleman and they both stepped into the road. He heard the warning shout and looked up to see a diligence approaching at a spanking trot. His instincts took over and he threw himself sideways taking the corpulent gentleman with him.

He landed on the pavement, the crashing fall knocking the wind out of his lungs. He rolled to one side and turned to see how the other pedestrian had fared.

'My word, that was a close one, and no mistake. I thank you,

Major. Without your prompt action we would both have perished beneath the wheels of that cart.'

'Are you unhurt, sir? Allow me to help you to your feet.' Jonathan had recovered sufficiently to stand up and he leaned over to offer his hand. Another gentleman assisted and together they got the corpulent man upright.

After a deal of backslapping and well-wishing he was eventually free to continue his journey, but his brush with death, caused by his own stupidity, had changed his mind. He no longer wished to get drunk. He would return to Grosvenor Square and spend every available moment at the side of the woman he was determined to step away from, however hard it might be for both of them.

He arrived at the house to find pandemonium. Kitty was sobbing and Adam looked grim. There was no sign of either Georgiana or Mary.

20

As the coach moved forward, Georgiana lashed out with her booted feet and was delighted to make contact with something solid and her kick elicited a snarl of protest. She tried again, but the response this time was for somebody's rough hands to grab her legs and these too were stuffed into a bag of some sort.

A glimmer of light filtered through the material over her head. If she could steady her breathing and blink the dust from her eyes, she might be able to see who was travelling in the vehicle with her. Whoever it was had not spoken and this made the situation even more unpleasant – if that were possible.

Her heart was hammering and she could scarcely catch her breath. Cold perspiration trickled down her neck and she bit her lip to stop a whimper. If she was to escape from this abduction unscathed, she must remain calm and be ready to take any opportunity that might arise.

The carriage was picking up speed and she was flung against the window. The sharp pain as her shoulder connected with the wooden frame cleared her head. She heard the coachman crack his whip and shout at his team.

They couldn't be going back onto Bond Street, for the road was congested; they must be travelling along Dover Street and would then turn into Piccadilly. Her knowledge of the streets of London faltered at this point, but she was fairly sure Chelsea was to the west, as was Green Park and St Martin-in-the-Fields. These areas were less populated. Wickham might have rented a house out there and this could be where she was being taken.

She had no doubt in her mind it was Wickham who had orchestrated this kidnapping. He had said he would get his revenge on her and Jonathan, and destroying her good name would be the perfect way to do it. Fitzwilliam would suffer too; he would blame himself for not being in London to protect her.

From the noxious odour drifting from the other side of the carriage, she was certain it was not Wickham who had done the actual abduction. There was only one person in the vehicle but she had no idea how many might be outside on the box.

If she lay quietly he might think she had swooned and would not pay her so much attention. The carriage was not travelling fast, presumably because the coachman did not wish to attract unwanted attention. If she could only wriggle free from the bags she was enveloped in, she might be able to roll from the carriage without injuring herself.

Unfortunately there was no opportunity as her journey ended far sooner than she'd anticipated. The vehicle slowed and then veered sharply left and rattled and bumped over uneven cobbles before it rocked to a standstill. There was little point in pretending she was asleep or unconscious as her captor prodded her sharply in the leg.

'I don't want no nonsense. I ain't got no time for the likes of you. Keep your mouth shut, missy, if you know what's good for you.' The voice matched the smell.

She mumbled her agreement and he appeared satisfied as he released the restriction around her legs and removed the sack from her head and shoulders. It was imperative that she heard and saw as much of her surroundings as possible – this information might be invaluable if she got the opportunity to flee.

The villain who had abducted her looked as repellent as he smelt and sounded. It took all of her courage not to shrink back into the corner and remain there. He pointed to the open door and she had no option but to scramble past him and blink into the sunlight.

She dare not make a point of looking around; she stood as if docile with her head lowered, but her eyes were darting about. Before she was rudely pushed in the small of her back and told to get a move on, she was able to discern the carriage was in a stable yard at the rear of a substantial, if dilapidated, old building. It was obvious she was no longer in the city, but somewhere on the outskirts, but not quite in the countryside.

She stumbled forward and made her way towards the open back door. She lifted her skirt in order to avoid tripping as she stepped over the threshold. This chamber was the kitchen, but not like any she had ever seen. There was no smart black range, merely an open fire above which trivets were suspended. There was no more than a moment to look round before she was bundled across the room and into the dark and dismal-smelling passageway.

'Get a move on; ain't got all day. You ain't the only one we got to nab today.'

Georgiana was relieved she wasn't going to be incarcerated in a cellar; at least he was chivvying her towards the front of the house. He pointed to a small, dark anteroom and she obediently stepped inside. The door slammed behind her, leaving her alone. She heard the sound of a key being turned and then her captor's footsteps faded away.

There had been no time to see if the room was furnished, and she was reluctant to move from her position inside the door until her vision adjusted to the darkness. Although the shutters were closed, a small amount of light filtered through the cracks in the wooden struts and, after a few minutes, she was able to pick out various shapes and identify them as a table, chair, and what could be a commode. On the far side, against the wall, was a narrow bed.

Her heart had returned to its normal, regular beat and she was more in control of the situation than she had been when she was being transported in the carriage. She walked to the window and attempted to open the shutters, but they had been nailed together; she would have to find something to prise off the pieces of wood that had been put across the gap if she wished to be able to see out of the window.

Maybe there was something she could use – she examined the table and chair, but they were solid and no amount of tugging and pulling made any difference. The legs and back of the chair remained firmly fixed together. Disappointed that her first attempt had ended in failure, she began a more thorough search of the chamber she had been imprisoned in.

The small wooden cupboard did indeed contain a chamber pot. She prayed fervently that she would not be obliged to use this as when doing so she would be in full view of anyone who cared to open the door; they had not thought to give her a screen for privacy.

The fireplace was empty. Wickham obviously didn't intend her to be comfortable during her incarceration. After a further half an hour of fruitless searching she abandoned the idea that she would be able to open the shutters. She sank onto the chair and, after putting her arms on the table, she dropped her head upon them in despair.

She closed her eyes and ran through the events of the morning, trying to make sense of them. Had Mary been involved in this plot and deliberately led her to the place where the carriage was waiting? The villain who had brought her here had said he had to capture a second person – she was at a loss to fathom out who the second victim might be.

Her mouth was dry; her stomach rumbled. It had been a long time since she had broken her fast. Then she jerked upright as something else occurred to her. Mary and Mr Colby must have seen her being abducted, but would they have alerted Jonathan and Adam to her disappearance? Although she and Mary had not become as close as she and Kitty had, she could not believe the girl would have betrayed her trust like this. No – Mary would definitely say what she had seen.

Adam and Jonathan were military men. They would know what to do and a rescue party would already be on its way to her. Was there anything she could do to cause Wickham problems? The door to the chamber opened inwards – if she could drag a few pieces of furniture across and pile them up against the doorway, this would delay anybody getting in. The fact that this meant she would also not be given anything to eat or drink was immaterial. She would be safe, and with luck would remain so until they arrived to rescue her.

If she was being realistic the chances of them finding her today were remote, but find her they would – of that she was certain – therefore she must keep herself safe until they did arrive. She shivered as an unwelcome thought slipped into her head.

Wickham intended to ruin her and to do that all he needed was for her to be found unchaperoned with an unmarried gentleman. This must be what her kidnapper was doing at the moment – he was fetching someone who would take her good name if he could get into this chamber and remain here all night. She refused to consider the possibility that whoever this unknown gentleman was would force his attentions on her. If that were to happen then no decent man would ever marry her – Jonathan would be lost to her forever.

This thought gave her the necessary impetus to leap to her feet and begin to build a barricade. The bed was cast iron and was difficult to move but eventually she dragged it across the boards and leant it against the door. She followed with the lumpy horsehair mattress, the table and the chair. She hastily removed the chamber pot from the cupboard and then added this to the inadequate pile she had assembled.

At least she was warm, if decidedly dirty, and had done the best she could to keep herself inviolate. If she sat on the chair then she would be adding her own weight to the barrier and this might make all the difference.

* * *

Jonathan took in the situation at a glance; he did not have to be told that something catastrophic had occurred, which involved both Georgiana and Mary.

'Adam, what the hell is going on here? Has that bastard got Georgiana? Where is Mary – surely he hasn't taken her too?'

'Come into the drawing room. We cannot discuss it out here.' Adam picked up his sobbing wife and carried her; she seemed incapable of saying anything sensible. Once they were safely inside and both doors were closed, he dumped Kitty on a chair and turned to face him.

'Kitty has no idea where the others are – it appears she was busy at the counter and then Ellie, Georgiana's maid, told her that her mistress had gone after Mary who had left the shop. That is the last time either girl was seen.'

'For God's sake, what about the two footmen who were to accompany her? Why didn't they do something?'

'The prince drove in an open carriage down Bond Street this morning and that caused chaos. The men who were supposed to be waiting at the door decided to join the gawping crowd to watch the carriage go past.'

'I take it they have been dismissed without reference?' If they hadn't, Jonathan decided he would deal with the matter himself.

'They have. They are collecting their belongings and will be off the premises within the hour. I have asked all the male staff to assemble in the hall and was about to organise a search.'

Jonathan crouched down beside the sobbing girl. 'Kitty, my dear, stop crying and talk to me. How long ago did you notice Mary and Georgiana had gone?' Whilst he waited for her to mop her eyes, he spoke directly to Adam. 'We need to speak to both maids; they might have seen something.'

He heard his friend move off and speak to somebody and knew the servants would be summoned immediately. Kitty had finally stopped crying.

'As soon as Ellie told me Georgiana had gone after my sister, I rushed to the door but I couldn't see either of them.' Her voice was barely above a whisper, and her eyes blotched and red. She paused and blew her nose loudly before continuing. 'I thought at first that the footmen had accompanied them, but then Ellie saw them staring down the road after the prince's carriage. I thought there was no point in searching myself, so I ran back and had only just arrived when you came in.'

'Thank you, sweetheart, none of this was your fault. Don't worry. Adam and I will find them.'

There was a sudden commotion outside and the doors flew open to reveal Mary, her cheeks tear-streaked and her bonnet askew. 'I cannot believe I was so taken in by him. They have stolen Georgiana. It is Wickham and Lydia who have taken her, as I recognised our carriage.'

Jonathan pointed to a chair and the girl collapsed on to it. She was visibly shaking and he hated having to interrogate her so fiercely. 'You had better tell us exactly how you were involved with this. There is no time to waste.'

'Mr Colby sent me a note asking me to meet him again in Dover Street and I slipped away, hoping I could be back before I was missed. It was just a ploy to draw Georgiana after me. Our stolen carriage was there the first time as well, but I didn't realise the significance until today. I was arguing about it with Mr Colby when something made me look over my shoulder and I saw Georgiana being snatched.'

'Go on – what happened next?'

'Mr Colby ran away, abandoning me on the pavement. I saw the carriage heading for Piccadilly, but I did not wait; then my maid and I ran all the way back to tell you what had happened.'

'What does the Bennet carriage look like?'

She recoiled at his sharp tone and swallowed nervously. 'It is painted dark blue and has brass lamps hanging on either side of the box. It was drawn by a team of bay horses.'

Jonathan exchanged a glance with his friend. Adam nodded. 'I shall find Colby, he is up to his neck in this and will not come out unscathed.'

The doors opened for a second time and the two maidservants were all but pushed into the drawing room. The girls had little else to add to what they already knew. From the racket outside the male members of staff were waiting for instructions.

Adam had already left to find Colby and would no doubt knock the information out of him if necessary. Jonathan would do the rest. He wished he had his pistols with him, but too late for regrets. He must manage with what he had.

'Kitty, take your sister to her bedchamber and make sure she remains there. She is to speak to no one. She will be returned to her parents in disgrace when this is over.' This was harsh, but Georgiana would not have been abducted without Mary's unwitting assistance.

He waited until the two girls had gone and then followed them. He faced the motley crew of inside and outside men, grooms, gardeners and footmen and gave them their orders.

'No doubt you are aware that Miss Darcy has been abducted by Mr Wickham. We know that the carriage was heading for Piccadilly, so we will begin our search that side of town. How many of you ride?'

An older man, dressed smartly in buff breeches and boots, stepped forward. 'We have eight horses, Major, plus your own mount. They are all being saddled.' He gestured to the five similarly garbed men standing in a group around him. 'These are stable hands and outriders, sir; we need only two more.'

Three footmen raised their hands and Jonathan selected the two youngest and fittest. 'You have five minutes to change and be outside ready to ride.' He dismissed the rest of the men before explaining to those remaining what he wished them to do.

'You—' he pointed to the man who had spoken '—I take it you are the head groom? What is your name?'

'Jarvis, Major, at your service.'

'Then, Jarvis, is there anyone amongst you who is familiar

with the area of the city to the west of Piccadilly? As far afield as Chelsea perhaps?'

Jarvis touched his forelock and nodded. 'I reckon I'm your man. I come from St Martin-in-the-Fields myself.'

'In which case, Jarvis, you take three of your best men and set off immediately. Do not make a parade of this; ride briskly but not in a way to draw attention to yourselves. Get your men to stop and ask passers-by if they saw a dark blue carriage drawn by two bays go past, and in which direction it was travelling.'

He had moved into a military frame of mind and viewed these men as his temporary soldiers. 'You must take cudgels, and be prepared to use them if necessary.'

Jarvis took three of the men and Jonathan snapped his fingers at the butler who was lurking in the background. 'The keys to the gun cupboard, now, if you please.'

Robinson held out his hand. 'I have them here, Major Brownstone, if you would care to follow me.'

Jonathan turned to the remaining couple of men. 'Either of you know how to handle a gun?'

'I can use a musket, sir; me pa showed me like,' one of them replied.

'Excellent, come with me. You—' he pointed to the other groom '—when the footmen return, get them outside and mounted. I shall wish to leave immediately I have the weapons I require.'

In less than ten minutes he was in the stable yard, two loaded and primed pistols in his pockets and a sword strapped behind him. When he rescued Georgiana he did not intend any of the perpetrators to survive the encounter.

21

Georgiana had no way of knowing how long she had been locked in this dismal room. The house was silent. She was almost certain there was nobody else inside – not even Wickham or his wife. Would it be safe to move to the window for a few moments and stare between the slats of the closed shutters?

It was impossible to make out any shapes, but the sun did seem to be lower in the sky so perhaps it was mid-afternoon already. While she was away from her position on the chair, she decided she had no option but to make use of the chamber pot.

After adjusting her clothing and returning to her seat, she resolved that if Wickham did manage to break through her makeshift barricade she would throw the contents of the pot in his face. The thought cheered her up. It was hardly a ladylike thing to do, but it would give her immense satisfaction.

If the bed was still usable she might have stretched out and slept – this at least would have passed the time. The room had become even chillier as the day progressed and she wished there were some blankets she could wrap around herself. The fact that nobody had bothered to bring her food or drink, nor to set a fire or provide her with covers or a pillow, meant whoever it was either did not intend to keep her long or... she could not complete this thought.

Wickham was an evil man, but was he so past redemption he would leave her to slowly starve to death? Thank God it was not winter or she would already be in distress. She pushed these morbid thoughts aside and concentrated on the notion that Jonathan and Adam would already be searching for her. That they would eventually find her she had no doubt, but would it be in time to save her from whatever fate Wickham had in store?

Another hour went by before Georgiana heard voices, and then heavy footsteps approached the door. She braced her feet on the floor and leaned back not a moment too soon. The key grated in the lock and someone threw their weight against it. Her barricade held. It shifted an inch or two but not enough to allow anyone to get in.

'Miss Darcy, would you be kind enough to move the obstruction so I can come in? I have your supper and unless the door is open you will remain cold and hungry.'

'Mr Wickham, I have no wish for your refreshments. I suggest that you remove yourself as Major Brownstone and Mr King will be here before long and I doubt you will escape their wrath.' She was pleased her voice sounded clear and fear had not made it tremble.

He swore and she flinched from the venom in his voice. He hurled himself against the door and she pushed back, just managing to keep things in place. He could not reach her through the windows as they were boarded up from the inside and now she was glad this had been done.

'Damn you to hell, I shall waste no further time here. Rawlings will be arriving momentarily and it matters not whether you actually stay in the same room – the damage will be done – you will have no option but to marry him tomorrow. You can be very sure that everyone in London already knows you have eloped with him. My wife has been busy spreading the tale. You are ruined, Miss Darcy, and so is your brother.'

'I care not what society says about me, Major Brownstone and my family will know it is untrue. I shall be married tomorrow – not to Mr Rawlings but to the man I love.' Brave words, as she wasn't sure even her beloved Jonathan would still wish to marry her if her reputation was gone.

There was the sound of smashing crockery – Wickham in his rage must have thrown the tray to the floor. She waited for him to try again to shift the door but it was quiet. He must have departed and the noise had drowned his footsteps. However she dare not move from her position, just in case he was bluffing.

If what Wickham had said was true, then her life might depend on her ability to keep the door closed until rescue arrived. She blinked back unwanted tears at the thought that Mr Rawlings, a young man from a good family, had become so depraved he was prepared to force her into an unwanted marriage. Were he to... Were he to force his attentions upon her, to violate her innocence, then her life would be over.

She would rather die than marry such a man. Would she have the courage to end her own life if the situation demanded it?

* * *

Jonathan had his guide lead him through the back streets until they reached the turning from which the stolen carriage must have emerged into Piccadilly. This route was thick with traffic; it would have been impossible for anyone to have picked out the Bennet carriage amongst so many others of similar colour and drawn by similar bay horses. He rode ahead of the other three, all of them scanning the traffic and the pedestrians in the hope of seeing someone they knew who might be able to help them with their search.

Once they were out of the congested area, there were fewer carriages, but also fewer pedestrians to ask. The men under his command dodged from side to side of the street, enquiring in a coffee house, a cobblers and a haberdashery, but to no avail.

Then one of the men gestured with his hand at a carriage approaching on the other side of the road. Jonathan's pulse quickened. This could be the Bennet carriage – it certainly fitted the description.

He had no wish to alarm the coachman so backed his horse into the passageway where he could not be seen. A man in dragoon blue was easily recognised and there wouldn't be many in this uniform around. From his position he gestured for two of the mounted men to hide themselves on the opposite side and then spoke to the groom who was with him. 'We need an obstruction – see that diligence waiting outside the coopers? Unhitch the team and take them across the road. Hurry, man, it needs to look like an accident and if we wait much longer the coachman will see us.'

He dismounted and dropped the reins on the ground in front of his gelding, hoping it would remain until he called him. He slid his hand into his pocket and carefully eased out the pistol. He had no wish for it to go off half-cocked.

The huge dray horses were obedient to the bit and it was a matter of moments before the cart was across the thoroughfare.

Fortunately there was no traffic in either direction at that moment, but it would not be long before there would be riders and drivers protesting at the delay.

An irate drayman appeared from the factory. 'Come 'ere, you – what you think you're doing? Bring me horses back this minute before I fetch the law on you.'

Jonathan moved in quickly behind him, before the man could create a hue and cry. 'I apologise for inconveniencing you, sir. Here is a florin for your trouble.' He offered no further explanation and the man, on receiving the coin, bit it to make sure it was not false, and then with a shrug, returned to whatever he had been doing inside the building.

Jonathan remained in the shadows, now the dark blue of his uniform was making him almost invisible unless a watcher actually knew he was there. The carriage rocked to a standstill and the coachman swore and cracked his whip. 'Get them beasts outa me way. I ain't got time to dally here.'

The groom made a fine pretence of being unable to shift the diligence and as Jonathan had hoped, the coachman tied the reins around the post, pulled on the brake and scrambled down to help back up the horses.

He ran across and flung open the door. 'Hands on your head. Do it now if you wish to live.'

The sole occupant was a malodorous, evil-looking creature with broken teeth and crawlers visible in his lank hair. Jonathan's sudden appearance with a loaded gun was enough to get the reaction he required. The man's hands shot to his head as if pulled by an invisible rope.

The far door was flung open and one of the footmen jumped in with a piece of twine in his hand. The man was soon trussed up like a pig going to market – he certainly smelt like one. The coachman had been similarly treated and was bundled head first into the vehicle, to land with a thump in the well of the carriage.

Jonathan slammed the door and leaned out of the window. 'One of you drive; the other bring the horses. Turn the vehicle and head in the direction it was coming from – I shall have the exact location in a short space of time.'

He was used to interrogating prisoners and doubted these two miscreants would resist for very long. He leaned forward, almost gagging at the stench, until his nose was almost touching the man on the seat opposite.

'Address. Now.' He slowly raised the pistol until it was resting against the man's filthy forehead. 'You will hang anyway, so I care naught if I end your life a few weeks earlier.'

He began to squeeze the trigger and that was all it took. 'Gag them, if you please. I have no wish for them to alert anybody they might have left guarding Miss Darcy.'

He banged on the roof and the carriage stopped. He handed the pistol to the groom and then jumped out and collected his horse. 'Follow me, and this time I care naught if we attract attention.'

He clicked his tongue and pressed his heels into the horse's flanks – it moved smoothly from standstill to canter and then extended its stride until they were galloping pell-mell down the street. Before they arrived at the place where he had been told his darling girl was waiting, Jarvis and the other three stable hands caught up with them.

There was no need to explain; it was obvious what was going on and like a cavalry charge the five of them thundered down the road. The house he wanted was set back behind a stand of trees and had a short drive that led to a stable yard at the rear of the property. The man had had no idea of the name of this place, but had said that it had twisted chimneys that were easily seen from the road.

He saw the building just ahead and gave the signal to slow their mad gallop. The carriage would arrive soon enough, but he had sufficient men to do what he had to in order to rescue Georgiana.

'Dismount, men, leave your horses in the adjacent field. Bring your cudgels, they might be needed. I have no idea how many we are facing – but it is best to be prepared. The bastard in the carriage said he had left the place empty but others were expected to arrive in his absence.'

He unhooked his riding cape and tossed it over the saddle, then untied the sword and scabbard and fastened it around his waist.

This was his element – he was comfortable with whatever might happen and was confident there would be a happy outcome.

'You will not speak. Watch my hands as I will use them to indicate what I wish you to do. Surprise is essential.'

He led them along the hedge that bordered the house until he found a place he and his troops could squeeze through. They were now behind the stable block and would be unobserved from the house. He loosened his sword in the scabbard and then belatedly remembered he had left the other pistol in his coat pocket. He glanced over his shoulder to see what weaponry they had – Jarvis and his men all held stout cudgels and he had his sword – that should be enough.

As they approached the rear of the stables, they could hear horses stamping inside. He raised his hand and everyone froze. He inched forward until he was level with an opening high on the wall. He gestured for Jarvis to step forward and provide him with a boost. The man obediently clasped his hands and

Jonathan placed his foot in them and was raised so he could peer through the aperture.

There were two horses inside, but no humans. He jumped down and held up two fingers indicating there were two horses and then shook his head. All four nodded, understanding what he was telling them. He moved smoothly forward until he was at the corner of the building, then pressed his back against the wall and glanced round.

He caught a flash of movement behind a grime-streaked window and thanked God he had taken the precaution of looking before he'd moved forwards. They would need to create a distraction and bring out whoever was inside, but it would have to appear innocent – he wasn't going to risk Georgiana being hurt. If Wickham knew he was being attacked, he might well gain his freedom by using her as a bargaining tool.

He gestured for the men to retreat and when he was certain they were out of earshot of the house, he explained what he wanted them to do. Once he was sure they understood, he returned to his place at the corner of the stables where he could watch the kitchen window.

Jarvis disappeared, taking two of the men with him, leaving one waiting silently behind him. Ten minutes went by before his plan was put into action. The sound of raised voices and the clattering of hooves at the front of the building indicated Jarvis and his men were doing as he'd requested.

He watched the window and was sure whoever had been there had now rushed to the front of the house to discover what the fuss was about. He had told Jarvis to unsaddle one of the horses and chase it up the drive as if it had escaped. He waited until he heard fresh voices joining in the shouting.

This was his chance. Crouching low, he sped across the cobbled yard and threw himself against the back door. It gave way beneath him and he all but tumbled into the flagstone passageway beyond. He steadied himself and his sword flashed in the darkness. The front door was open – whoever was here had exited that way. He pointed and mimed that his companion should bolt the door behind them.

He stopped and closed the back door – he had burst the bolts so he couldn't stop the men outside from entering. He had only a few moments to find Georgiana and make sure she was safe. He was about to race upstairs, when he heard her calling him from the far end of the passageway.

In seconds he was at the door and turned the key, but he could not shift it more than an inch. 'Sweetheart, are you unhurt? Quickly, move whatever you have put behind this door and come out to me.'

'I knew you would come. It is Wickham who is here and he has another with him.' The noise she was making hurling furniture about would attract attention very soon.

He was leaning his whole weight against the door when suddenly it shifted and she was through the gap and in his arms. He crushed her to his chest and she clung to him.

'Major, I reckon the varmint's heard us and is on his way back. He tried the front and now he's going round the back.'

'Take Miss Darcy out through the front and get her to safety. I will deal with Wickham and his accomplice.'

Georgiana refused to budge. 'You must not kill him; promise me you will not kill him.'

For a moment he was tempted to refuse, but the need to get his beloved safe was more important than getting the satisfaction of ending Wickham's miserable existence.

'I give you my word. Now, do as you're told, and get out of here.' He shoved her none too gently in the direction of the front door, which was now open. She picked up her skirts and raced down the corridor not a moment too soon.

As the door slammed shut behind her, so Wickham and his henchmen burst in. Jonathan had made a catastrophic misjudgement. Both men were armed with pistols and both were pointing at his heart.

22

Georgiana was half dragged across the grass; the man who had her arm was determined to take her away from Jonathan. While she was struggling to free herself, the Bennet carriage arrived in the drive and a loose horse clattered past the railings that fronted the property. She stopped and watched in amazement as the coachman, and a man from inside, dropped to the ground before the vehicle was quite stationary. They raced to the rear of the building and both were holding weapons.

Whilst the groom holding her arm was distracted, she wrenched herself free and headed back to the house. As she reached the front door there was the hideous crack of a gun being fired followed immediately by three more retorts.

Ignoring the cries for her to wait she burst into the hallway to see Jonathan was upright, but there were two bodies face down on the boards. The two from the coach were holding smoking guns and the air was heavy with the smell of explosives.

Thank God! Her beloved was unscathed. She ran to him and

as she reached his side his eyes blazed for a second and then seemed to dim.

'Forgive me, my darling, it should not have ended like this.'

His eyes closed and to her horror his knees appeared to crumple and he slowly slid down the wall, leaving a dreadful trail of blood behind him. He had been shot and she hadn't realised. She dropped to her knees beside his unconscious figure and only then saw the bloodstained bullet hole in his uniform jacket.

For a moment she was frozen but then common sense took over. He was bleeding from his back so the bullet must have gone through – she must stop the bleeding, as loss of blood could prove fatal. Ignoring the men who were crowding into the hallway, she began to rip strips from her petticoat. Someone knelt beside her and together they made a pad of material and Jarvis, for she recognised him now, groped inside Jonathan's jacket and pressed it on the entry wound.

'Here, miss, give me the other one and I'll put it at the back. You tear off some more strips to bind them in place.'

She couldn't speak, but nodded her agreement. By the time they had the bandages in place, four men she recognised from Grosvenor Square appeared at their side with a trestle upon which to carry Jonathan to the carriage.

'I've sent a man ahead, Miss Darcy, to raise the alarm and there will be a doctor waiting when we arrive.'

Georgiana needed to use the wall to get herself upright again. She stood to one side as Jonathan was carefully lifted onto the trestle and then picked up. Only then did she glance at the bodies – one of them was Wickham – she recognised his fair curls. She was glad he was dead; after what he had done to Jonathan she would willingly have shot him through the heart herself.

Outside the sun still shone, everyday noises filled the air, but she heard none of it. Her attention was concentrated on the unconscious form of the man she could not live without. She arrived at the side of the carriage as they were carefully manhandling him inside.

Jarvis touched her arm politely. 'I reckon you'll be better coming up with me, miss. The stench in there is something rank.' He gestured towards two bound prisoners tossed against the hedge like unwanted sacks of rubbish. 'They were in...'

She stepped around Jarvis and was inside before he could argue. Jonathan was too tall to lie across the squabs but was propped with his feet on the floor and his torso on the seat. Without hesitation she lifted his head and wriggled beneath it, then settled him comfortably on her lap.

The door slammed and the coach moved off without further conversation. Every jolt, every jerk of the carriage was increasing the risk. Despite the bandages Jonathan was bleeding profusely – there was an unpleasant stickiness seeping out onto her gown.

She prayed as she had never done before that God would spare him, that somehow there would be a miracle and he would open his eyes and everything would be all right. The journey seemed interminable. Although they were travelling at an indecent pace, it was not fast enough. Unless Jonathan received sutures in his wounds very soon, he would surely bleed to death.

Eventually they were home. The door was flung open and Adam was inside the carriage. 'My God, what a dreadful thing to happen. Do not look so concerned, little one, the major will not give up easily. He has everything to live for.'

He reached across and pushed her hair out of her eyes. 'Are you well? Were you hurt in any way?'

'I was not, and Wickham is dead. Is the doctor here?'

'He is. Let me take over now; we must get him inside immediately.'

Georgiana allowed Adam to take hold of Jonathan's limp shoulders and then three other male servants were there to assist, and her beloved was gone, leaving her to find her own way from the carriage. She closed her eyes and tears trickled down her cheeks. She wished Fitzwilliam was here – he would know what to do.

For some reason she was unable to stir herself. Her limbs were heavy; it was as if she was being weighed down by an invisible force. Then she was vaguely aware that Adam had returned and lifted her gently from the seat. There was nothing more she could do; Jonathan's life was in the hands of the Almighty and the skill of the physician attending him.

'Here we are, sweetheart, Ellie will soon have you warm and comfortable.' Adam placed her in an armchair and then was gone again.

The chatter of her maids was a comfort but Georgiana paid no attention and made no response. However, when she was guided into a warm, scented bath she began to revive. 'I need to wash my hair. I feel tainted by where I have been and will not be happy until I am free of the smell.'

'Mrs King is waiting to speak to you in your sitting room, miss. Will you be getting dressed or putting on your nightgown?'

'It is scarcely bedtime, Ellie. I shall get dressed again of course. Would you be kind enough to tell Mrs King I will see her as soon as I am ready?'

* * *

Kitty greeted her with a fierce embrace. 'Dearest Georgiana, I am so pleased to see you home and unhurt. I find it hard to comprehend that Wickham shot Jonathan. What a horrible thing to happen – I imagine that my mother is having a conniption fit at the thought of having her son-in-law labelled an abductor and murderer.'

'It is better that Wickham is dead. Having him on the gallows would have been so much worse. I must go and see how Jonathan is doing. Forgive me, but I cannot linger here.' Georgiana embraced her friend again and hurried out.

The guest rooms were on the other side of the house and she made her way there with a feeling of dread. The fact that no one had come to see her after the doctor had visited was not a good sign, in her opinion. She burst into the sitting room of Jonathan's apartment without knocking, but it was empty.

She rushed across the room and opened the bedroom door expecting to find Adam, the doctor and a nurse in there as well as her darling Jonathan. This room was also empty apart from the still figure in the centre of the bed. For a second her heart almost stopped beating – then she realised his face was not covered – so he could not be dead.

Why was there no one here to watch over him? She moved quietly to the bed and to her astonishment and delight he turned his head and smiled at her.

'You have taken an unconscionable time to get here, sweetheart. I thought you would be at my bedside long ago.'

Somewhat taken aback by his comment, she stared at him, wondering if his wits were addled by the loss of blood. 'In case you have forgotten, Major Brownstone, I was kidnapped earlier today and had to scrub myself from head to toe in order to remove any vermin I might have picked up. I have not eaten since early this morning, neither have I had a drink – but here I am at your bedside. I can see that I need not have bothered if you are perfectly well.'

Instead of answering her, he reached across and took her hand in a surprisingly strong grip. 'You are a pea-goose, my love, I was attempting a feeble jest, but I can see I sadly missed the mark.'

'I thought you were going to die; you had a hole shot right through you and...'

'I have no wish to talk about what happened to me. I am a soldier. I have been wounded before and will be on my feet in no time.'

'How is your wound? When I saw you an hour or so ago you were unconscious and as white as a ghost.'

'I have a prodigious number of stitches but as far as the doctor knows the bullet caused no serious damage. I am to drink as much watered wine as I can stomach, rest in bed for a day or two, and then I shall be fine.'

He gave her hand a tug. 'I sent everyone away so we could be alone. I am sorry that I teased you; it was a stupid thing to do. We have much to talk about, sweetheart, and it would be so much easier if you sat next to me on the bed.'

How could she refuse such a request? There was no need for him to shift as he was already in the centre of the huge bed. A sudden impulse made her kick off her indoor slippers and scramble up beside him. Instead of sitting demurely on the edge, she stretched out on top of the coverlet and rested her head on his sound shoulder.

With a sigh of satisfaction he pulled her indecently close and then his breathing deepened. He had fallen asleep. Her stomach gurgled and she was eager to find some refreshment, but she would remain within his embrace and enjoy the closeness. She cared not for etiquette or reputation; they could both have died today and she was not going to let him out of her sight ever again.

This is what it would be like when they were married, lying next to him hearing him breathing, feeling the warmth of his body pressed against hers. It had been a long and difficult day – perhaps it would not hurt if she slept for a little while too.

* * *

When she opened her eyes the room was dark, but the fire had been lit in the grate and this made it possible to see a little. Jonathan was sleeping soundly, his breathing even and regular, and when she touched his cheek it was warm and firm beneath her fingers.

Someone had covered her with a blanket and she was almost too comfortable to move. Then she became aware there was someone else in the room.

'Georgiana dearest, you are awake at last. You must be sharp-set. I shall send for a tray immediately.'

The familiar voice filled her with joy. 'Fitzwilliam, how are you here so soon?' She carefully pushed back the cover and slithered out of the bed, making sure she did not disturb the other occupant.

Her brother was now on his feet and she threw herself into his arms. He gathered her close and then kissed her on top of her head. 'We must go next door and let the major sleep.'

Once they were in the sitting room and the door half-closed, he explained how he came to be there so quickly, told her about the dreadful letter Wickham had sent, and she explained exactly what had transpired that day.

'I did not see Mr Rawlings at all. Are you quite sure he was involved in this?'

'I fear that he was, but reluctantly so. He owed Wickham a small fortune in gambling debts and was persuaded that he could come about if he married you. King dealt with him and he is now on his way to his parents. No doubt they will pack him off to the colonies where he can do no further harm to us.'

'Adam told Mary she would be sent back to Longbourn in disgrace. It is no more than she deserves. Even if she did not intend for me to be abducted, she behaved disgracefully.' Georgiana had no wish to see the girl ever again.

'She will be leaving first thing tomorrow. I believe that Mr Bennet will not be so lenient with his daughter in future. She has learnt a valuable lesson and fortunately you were not harmed.'

Georgiana surged to her feet, anger making her forget her manners. 'How can you say that? I could have been forced to marry Mr Rawlings or worse, Jonathan could be dead – and all this happened because of her. I shall never forgive her and cannot understand why you are not as angry as I am.'

The supper tray was brought in and the conversation halted until they were alone again. The appetising smells coming from the tray made her remember just how hungry she was. Once she was replete, her good humour was restored and she was no longer filled with rage.

'Thank you, that was quite delicious. I apologise for my outburst; I am more composed now.'

'There is no need to apologise, sweetheart. What happened to you was unforgivable. It's a damn good thing that Wickham is dead, for I would have seen him dance on the end of a rope otherwise and that would be so much worse for the family.'

'What about Lydia Wickham? I did not see her at the house.'

'Lizzy and Jane both want me to be kind to her despite the fact that she behaved so abominably at Pemberley. She is little more than a schoolgirl, three years your junior, and yet she has been married and widowed already. What chance did she have when she was so spoiled and petted by her silly mother and then under the pernicious influence of Wickham? Mrs Bishop, the major's cousin, has offered to take Lydia under her care. She has family in India and intends to go for a long visit. With luck the girl will find herself another husband and not come back to plague us ever again.'

'That is a satisfactory arrangement, Fitzwilliam. I hesitate to suggest it, but would it be possible to settle a little money on her so she might make a decent marriage next time?'

He smiled and nodded. 'I have already put matters in motion, my dear, and as you know, have already done the same for Mary and will not retract my offer despite her reprehensible actions today.' He poured himself a third cup of coffee and she took one too, then he stretched out his booted legs and viewed her through narrowed eyes.

'I had an interesting conversation with Major Brownstone whilst you were elsewhere. It would seem he has a special licence in his pocket, and he has two weeks' leave so that you can get married immediately.'

Her cheeks burned and she could not meet his gaze. 'He might be away for years, Fitzwilliam, and I intend to be his wife before he leaves.'

'Do you indeed?' He laughed and she looked up, surprised he found the situation amusing. 'I should think you do, after spending the afternoon in his bed.'

'You will give your permission?'

'Not only that, my dear, I positively insist that you tie the knot as soon as may be. Kitty and her husband have no wish to remain in London – the ball has been cancelled – and you can be married with everyone who matters at your side.'

'It is amazing that there will be two weddings at Pemberley so close together and then three babies will arrive in a few weeks. I don't believe there have been any such events there in living memory.'

'Are you quite sure you wish to go ahead? I was not serious when I said you must get married. I am well aware that nothing untoward took place, and I do not wish you to rush into something you might regret.'

'I would regret not marrying him, Fitzwilliam. If he is killed in France then at least I will have happy memories to help me through the rest of my life.' She had been about to say that if God was willing she might also have a son or daughter by him to carry on his name. She thought that her brother might not appreciate hearing such an inappropriate remark from his sibling.

23

Jonathan awoke feeling weak, but no longer as if his head was stuffed with wool. The fact that his bedchamber was empty must mean everybody thought he was on the road to recovery. If he didn't jar his right arm at all then he was fairly sure he could roll out of bed. He had a desperate need and had no wish to embarrass himself with a messy accident.

He was exhausted by the time he had swung his legs to the floor and his head was swimming again. Then what he had thought was a shadow in an armchair by the fire, became a figure.

'Do not try to get out of bed, old fellow, without my assistance.' Darcy was at his side in a flash and supported him whilst he staggered to the screen behind which the necessary item was discreetly positioned.

'How are you here so soon? The letter Adam sent could not possibly have arrived.' Jonathan was relieved to be back in bed – he was not as fit as he had thought.

'I will tell you how I am here, but first I shall ring for a supper tray. Cook and several other members of staff have volunteered to remain up so they can provide you with anything you want.'

'I am devilishly hungry, but have no wish to be served gruel or broth – have something substantial sent up, if you please.'

Darcy had just finished recounting the events that had brought him to London, and everything else that had been organised whilst he was *hors de combat*, when a supper tray arrived. There was more than enough to feed two hungry men and by the time he was replete Jonathan was ready to broach a tricky subject.

'Darcy, no doubt Georgiana has told you the reasons for us marrying so suddenly. Do we have your blessing and consent?'

'It is not what I would wish for my sister, but I can refuse you nothing. You almost lost your life on her account, and I shall be eternally grateful. Yes, reluctantly, I give you my blessing and consent.'

This was all Jonathan wanted to know before telling his future brother-in-law what he had decided to do. 'Thank you, but there is going to be a change of plan. I doubt my sword arm will ever be the same – I know I could fight with my left – but I will never be the soldier I was. I intend to resign my commission and remain in England. Georgiana and I can be married as planned in September – there is no need for this unseemly rush.'

'Good man! I have been praying for that outcome ever since you and Georgiana became betrothed. I have three estates within an hour of Pemberley and you can take your pick. There are tenants in two of them but I can terminate the lease for whichever one you prefer.'

'We will take the house that is vacant – I have no wish to have anyone thrown out on my account. I have a few thousand in the funds – that should be sufficient to pay the rent.'

'Devil take it, man, I was not intending to rent you the property, but give it to you as a wedding gift. The place has been run by my estate manager and is the nearest of the three. As the house has been unoccupied for several years it will need refurbishment – but I'm sure Georgiana will enjoy doing that.'

Jonathan could not prevent a jaw-cracking yawn from escaping. He was damned tired and could scarcely keep his eyes open. 'I must sleep, Darcy. I shall be more the thing in the morning.'

'I bid you goodnight, and shall leave you to give my sister the good news when she visits.'

The room was quiet again, only the crackling of the fire to keep him company. Jonathan's mouth curved. Who would have thought so much could have happened in less than a day? He yawned again and carefully manoeuvred himself until he was prone once more.

He was in that delightful state between sleep and waking when the bed dipped and before he could protest his beloved was snuggling up against him – this time beneath the covers and if he was not mistaken she was not wearing a gown.

'Georgiana, what the hell are you doing here? Have you run mad? Your brother will run me through if he finds you in bed with me.'

'I heard you tell him your plans – I have no wish to wait until September to marry you and after this I doubt that even Fitzwilliam will think an immediate ceremony is not essential.' She giggled and snuggled dangerously close. 'I discarded my gown in your dressing room – I thought it would look more authentic if I was in my undergarments. It has been a very long day; I shall sleep now, but cannot wait to see the shock on the face of your valet when he brings in your shaving water. Goodnight, my darling, I love you so much and cannot wait to be your true wife.'

'And I love you, sweetheart, but I think it would be better for you to return to your chamber—' His words were useless as she relaxed and was instantly asleep. Her soft curves rested against him. Having her so close was going to take all his resolve if he were not to pre-empt their wedding night. He sighed. Despite being tired he doubted he was going to get much sleep.

ABOUT THE AUTHOR

Fenella J. Miller is the bestselling writer of over eighteen historical sagas. She also has a passion for Regency romantic adventures and has published over fifty to great acclaim. Her father was a Yorkshireman and her mother the daughter of a Rajah. She lives in a small village in Essex with her British Shorthair cat.

Sign up to Fenella J. Miller's mailing list for news, competitions and updates on future books.

Visit Fenella's website: www.fenellajmiller.co.uk

Follow Fenella on social media here:

facebook.com/fenella.miller
x.com/fenellawriter

ALSO BY FENELLA J MILLER

Goodwill House Series

The War Girls of Goodwill House

New Recruits at Goodwill House

Duty Calls at Goodwill House

The Land Girls of Goodwill House

A Wartime Reunion at Goodwill House

Wedding Bells at Goodwill House

A Christmas Baby at Goodwill House

The Army Girls Series

Army Girls Reporting For Duty

Army Girls: Heartbreak and Hope

Army Girls: Behind the Guns

Army Girls: Operation Winter Wedding

The Pilot's Girl Series

The Pilot's Girl

A Wedding for the Pilot's Girl

A Dilemma for the Pilot's Girl

A Second Chance for the Pilot's Girl

The Nightingale Family Series

A Pocketful of Pennies

A Capful of Courage

A Basket Full of Babies

A Home Full of Hope

At Pemberley Series

Return to Pemberley

Trouble at Pemberley

Scandal at Pemberley

Danger at Pemberley

Harbour House Series

Wartime Arrivals at Harbour House

Standalone Novels

The Land Girl's Secret

The Pilot's Story

You're cordially invited to

The Scandal Sheet

The home of swoon-worthy historical romance from the Regency to the Victorian era!

Warning: may contain spice 🌶

Sign up to the newsletter
https://bit.ly/thescandalsheet

Boldwood

Boldwood Books is an award-winning fiction publishing company seeking out the best stories from around the world.

Find out more at www.boldwoodbooks.com

Join our reader community for brilliant books, competitions and offers!

Follow us
@BoldwoodBooks
@TheBoldBookClub

Sign up to our weekly deals newsletter

https://bit.ly/BoldwoodBNewsletter

Printed in Dunstable, United Kingdom